D0065538

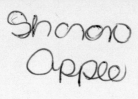

Sharon
Applee

THE BOBBSEY TWINS
AND THE GREEK HAT MYSTERY

A strange note in a fur hat—two Greek words and a drawing of a bull's horns! That's all it takes to arouse the curiosity of the Bobbsey Twins.

If a square white box had not fallen off a speeding bicycle —if the twins had not located the owner and returned the box—if a letter from Athens had not arrived at that very moment—the Bobbseys' surprise visit to Greece would not have been enhanced by mystery.

A tour of the Acropolis in Athens is very exciting, but exploring the ruins of the ancient palace of Knossos in Crete proves to be even more so. Here, Flossie is lost in its puzzling labyrinth, and Freddie uncovers a valuable tiny bronze chariot in a deep stone pit.

En route to Delphi, Bert observes a familiar-looking bundle of fur in a truck found smashed against a boulder, and Nan finds herself directly in the path of a huge rock which comes hurtling down the mountainside.

You will enjoy the added flavor of a foreign land as the adventurous Bobbsey Twins stumble upon another mystery while attempting to solve the one they have brought with them from Lakeport.

THE BOBBSEY TWINS
By Laura Lee Hope

The little wagon flipped over and
Freddie was sent sprawling!

The Bobbsey Twins and the Greek Hat Mystery

By

LAURA LEE HOPE

GROSSET & DUNLAP
Publishers   *New York*

The Bobbsey Twins and the Greek Hat Mystery

CONTENTS

Bert reached the package a split second before Danny

CHAPTER I

THE NOTE IN THE HAT

"LOOK, Bert!" Nan Bobbsey exclaimed. "A box fell off that bicycle!" She pointed to a square white package which lay in the middle of the street. A boy on a bicycle was just disappearing around the corner.

"Hey!" Bert called after the rider. "Wait! You dropped something!"

Bert and Nan were the twelve-year-old Bobbsey twins. They were tall and slender with dark hair and eyes.

Bert's call did not reach the bicycle rider. But two boys who were walking on the other side of the street looked up. One was Danny Rugg and the other Jack Westley. They were in the same grade at school as Bert and Nan. Danny and Jack were not very popular because they liked to play mean tricks on the other children.

When he spotted the box in the street Danny began to run. "I'll get it!" he called.

1

Bert, too, had dashed to pick up the box. He reached it a split second before Danny.

"That's mine, Bert Bobbsey!" the bully shouted. "I saw it first!"

"You didn't even notice it until you heard Bert call," Nan protested. "Anyway, the box doesn't really belong to either of you. It belongs to the boy on the bicycle!"

"Finders keepers!" Danny declared. "I found it, and I'm going to keep it!"

"Well you don't have it, so you can't keep it!" Bert said flatly. "Besides, I'll try to find out who lost it."

"I don't believe you!" Danny sneered. But he walked away and joined his pal on the sidewalk.

Bert and Nan hurried toward their home, keeping their eyes peeled for the bike rider. "I hope we can find out who that boy is," Nan said. "He's going to feel bad when he finds his package gone."

"I'd sure like to know what's in it," Bert said curiously. "It looks like a bakery box."

When the twins reached the large, comfortable house where the Bobbsey family lived, two blond, curly-haired children raced to meet them. They were the younger Bobbsey twins, six-year-old Freddie and Flossie.

"Where've you been?" cried Freddie, "Flossie and I got home 'way before you!"

"A boy lost this box off the back of his bicycle," Nan explained, "and Bert picked it up!"

"Not without a little argument with Danny," Bert added with a grin.

"What is it?" Flossie asked.

"We don't know," Nan replied. "Let's take it into the house and see if we can find a name anywhere."

Bert carried the box into the living room and put it on a table. Then the children examined the package carefully. There was no name or address visible.

"Open it, Bert!" Flossie urged, squirming with curiosity.

Bert turned questioningly to his twin. She nodded. "I think you'll have to! Maybe the name's inside."

They all leaned forward to look as Bert untied the string and lifted the lid of the square box.

"Ooh!" Flossie exclaimed. "Cakes!"

The box was filled with little sugar-covered pieces of pastry.

At that moment a jolly-looking colored woman came into the room. She was Dinah Johnson, who had helped Mrs. Bobbsey with the housework ever since the twins were little. Her

husband Sam worked in Mr. Bobbsey's lumber-
yard on the shore of Lake Metoka. The couple
lived on the third floor of the Bobbsey home.

Dinah peered at the contents of the box.
"What's the matter?" she asked, pretending to
frown. "Don't you like my cakes any more?
What you doin' buyin' things at a bakery?"

Flossie threw her arms around Dinah. "We
love your cakes, Dinah!" she said.

"Yes, 'specially the choc'late ones!" Freddie
agreed.

Quickly Nan explained that she and Bert had
seen the package fall from a bicycle and wanted
to take it back to its owner. "But we don't know
how to find him," she ended sadly.

Dinah looked at the cakes again. "They're
kinda queer-looking," she commented. "I never
saw any like them before."

"Maybe Mother knows what they are," Bert
suggested as a slender, pretty woman walked
into the room.

Again Nan explained about the cakes. Her
mother picked up the box. "Why, they're *baklava!*" she exclaimed. "They must have come
from the Greek bakery on Main Street. I don't
think anyone else in Lakeport makes cakes like
these."

"Call up the bakery, Bert," Nan urged.

"They'll probably know who bought the baklava."

Bert made the call. When he returned to the living room he looked relieved and explained that the cakes had been ordered by a Mr. Karilis, who owned the fur shop downtown. "I told the baker I'd deliver the cakes we found," Bert said.

"Oh, let's all go!" cried Flossie.

Lakeport was a small town and the twins often walked to the center by themselves. They had seen the fur shop but had never been inside.

As they pushed open the door a bell tinkled. A man came into the room from a door at the rear. He was of medium height with dark hair and a friendly smile.

"What can I do for you young ladies and gentlemen?" he asked. "I am Mr. Karilis."

Bert introduced himself and the others, then said, holding out the white bakery box, "We think this belongs to you. It fell off the delivery bicycle, and I picked it up."

"My baklava!" the man exclaimed. "I ordered it for my wife's birthday as a surprise. I am very glad you found it."

Nan had been looking around the shop. There were several beautiful fur coats on mannequins, and smaller fur pieces draped over the backs of the chairs.

Mr. Karilis spoke to her. "You like my furs?"

"Oh yes! They're lovely!" Nan sighed.

"Most of the coats and other things were made right here, back in my workroom," the man said proudly. "My grandfather, my father, my brother and I have all worked with furs. My grandfather and my father, they are gone now. But my brother Yannis, he has a small fur factory in our hometown—Athens, Greece."

"You were born in Greece?" Bert asked. "We're studying about it in school."

"Where is Greece?" Freddie spoke up.

Mr. Karilis pointed to a large map of the world which hung on one wall. "You see the Mediterranean Sea here between Europe and Africa?"

The twins nodded eagerly.

"This piece of land reaching into the Mediterranean just east of Italy is Greece."

"And you came all the way to Lakeport from there!" Flossie was astonished.

"It's not so far nowadays by plane," the furrier assured her. "My wife and I were in Greece just a month ago on our vacation."

"I'd sure like to go there sometime," Bert remarked.

Mr. Karilis turned toward a large carton which stood on the floor near the rear of the room. "These fur hats came just today from my brother's factory in Athens. We will sell them next fall."

He pulled out some wrapping paper and then a round hat of dark fur. With a smile he dropped the hat on Freddie's head. "How do you like that?" the man asked teasingly.

Freddie grinned and pulled the hat down over his eyes. The next minute he yanked it off. "That hurts!" he cried.

Bert took the headgear and felt it. "No wonder—there's something stiff in the lining," he said, handing the hat to the furrier.

"Very strange!" Mr. Karilis took a small pair of scissors from his pocket and opened a seam. Then he pulled out a piece of paper. "This looks like an address label!"

"There's a picture on it," Flossie pointed out.

Mr. Karilis put the paper down on the table and they all bent to look at it. In thick, black brush strokes someone had drawn a figure.

After it were the words *tessera epta.*

"What does it mean?" Nan asked curiously.

"That figure is the symbol for the horns of a

bull," Mr. Karilis replied. "It was used in ancient Greece. The words are Greek for *four* and *seven*. But I don't understand what this paper means or why it was in the lining of the hat!"

"It's a mystery!" Flossie decided.

The Bobbsey twins loved mysteries and were very good at solving them. In *The Big River Mystery* they had helped catch some smugglers on the Hudson River and had found their Aunt Alice's missing heirlooms.

"Perhaps my foreman can solve it for us," Mr. Karilis said. "Jim!" he called. "Will you come here, please?"

A thin little man entered from the workroom. Mr. Karilis introduced the children to him, then showed him the mysterious paper. "Have you any idea what this is about?"

The foreman gave the drawing a startled look, then shook his head.

"Maybe there are more papers in the other hats," Freddie suggested, reaching into the carton and picking up another fur headpiece.

Together, he and Mr. Karilis pulled out the packing paper from the case and felt the remaining hats. They found nothing unusual.

"Let's look at that paper again," the furrier said finally. He turned to the table, but the mysterious label was gone!

"Jim!" he called to the foreman, who had

gone back to the workroom with a bundle of packing paper in his arms. "Did you take that note?"

The foreman appeared in the doorway. "I didn't take note," he said. "I just clear bunch of paper from table. Maybe note was mixed up with it and is burning in incinerator now. I did not know you wanted to keep it."

Mr. Karilis frowned, then shrugged. "Well, I guess it doesn't really matter," he said. "It was probably just some kind of joke."

As the children said good-by and turned to leave the fur shop, the front door opened and the postman came in. "Lots of letters for you today," he said cheerfully and handed a packet of mail to Mr. Karilis.

The furrier hurriedly shuffled through the pile. "Here's one from my brother in Athens," he said. "Perhaps he will have something to say about that strange piece of paper you found, Freddie."

The children waited while he slit open the envelope and began to read. They were startled when Mr. Karilis gasped, "Oh no!" and then sank into a chair.

"Is something wrong?" Nan asked quickly.

"My furs have been stolen!" was the reply.

CHAPTER II

THE BULL JUMPERS

"YOUR furs!" Nan repeated in surprise, looking around the room. "What do you mean?"

"The small pieces of fur I sent back to Greece," Mr. Karilis replied. "They have been stolen."

The fur man explained that the paws and other bits of fur which were left over from the making of coats were collected, packed into large bales, and then shipped to Greece.

"The workers in my brother's factory cut these pieces into tiny strips," Mr. Karilis continued. "Next they are sewn together again into larger pieces which we call 'plates' and shipped back to me. We use the plates to make fur coats and hats."

Flossie giggled. "A hat made of plates would look funny!" she said.

"If you fell down, you'd break your hat!" Freddie put in.

10

With a smile Mr. Karilis reminded the small twins that these particular plates were made of fur, not china. "It is very sad that the bale of fur was stolen because without it, the workers will have nothing to do and will lose their jobs!" he went on.

"How was the bale stolen?" Bert asked.

Mr. Karilis read his brother's letter more carefully. "Yannis says that he sent a workman named Thanos in the truck to Piraeus to pick up the fur from the ship. He got the bale but never came back to the factory!"

"How awful!" Nan cried.

"Where's Piraeus?" Freddie asked.

"It is the main port of Greece, about six miles from Athens," the fur man explained. "All the ships from America dock there."

"Doesn't your brother have any idea where Thanos might have gone?" Bert queried.

"No. He says the police are still trying to find him."

"If we could go to Greece, we'd solve the mystery!" Freddie declared.

Mr. Karilis smiled. "Well, you've solved one mystery for me," he said. "You found the lost baklava. Thank you very much!"

As the children walked home they talked about the theft. "I'm so sorry for those people in the factory who won't have any work," Nan said.

"I hope the police find the bale of fur soon."

"It's too bad the mystery is in Greece," Bert added. "If the fur had been stolen here in Lakeport, we could have had fun working on the case."

That evening the children told their parents about their visit to the fur shop.

"It's a shame Mr. Karilis is having such trouble," Mrs. Bobbsey said sympathetically. "I've met Mrs. Karilis. She is a very nice woman."

"Mr. Karilis is nice too!" Flossie spoke up. "And you know what? He makes hats out of plates!" she said, grinning impishly.

Nan was explaining about the fur "plates" when the telephone rang. Dinah answered and called Mrs. Bobbsey. When she returned she was smiling.

"That was Mrs. Karilis calling," the twins' mother said. "She says her husband thought you children might like to see some pictures of Greece since you seemed so interested in that country this afternoon."

"I sure would!" Bert said quickly. He had a camera of his own and was always eager to see other people's pictures.

"Yes, let's go!" Freddie jumped up from his chair and headed for the door.

"Wait a minute there, my little fat fireman!" Mr. Bobbsey called. This was his nickname for his younger son. Ever since he had been a very little boy, Freddie had declared he was going to be a fireman when he grew up. A toy fire engine was his favorite plaything.

"You're invited for tomorrow afternoon," Mrs. Bobbsey said when Freddie came back to the table. "I said I thought you could come right after lunch since it'll be Saturday."

"I can't wait," Flossie said happily. "I like to look at pictures."

Early the next afternoon the four twins made their way to the Karilis home. It was a white frame house set back from the street. Mrs. Karilis greeted them warmly.

When Nan remarked about the pretty house, Mrs. Karilis laughed and said, "It is difficult for us to get used to living in a wooden house. All our homes in Greece are made of stone, since there are many rocks and few trees."

Mr. Karilis was busy setting up the screen and projector in the living room. He shook hands with each of the children and showed them where to sit.

"I'll get the slides," Mrs. Karilis said, starting toward the door.

Flossie jumped up. "I'll carry them for you," she volunteered.

"That will be very nice," their hostess agreed. "Come along."

She led the way into a smaller room. On a

Flossie and the slides fell to the floor!

table at one side were several boxes of slides. Flossie ran over and gathered the boxes up in her arms.

"Can you carry them all?" Mrs. Karilis asked.

"Oh yes," the little girl replied.

Her arms full, Flossie ran into the living room where the others were waiting. The next instant she caught her foot in the electric cord which ran from the projector to the wall. *Crash!* Flossie and the boxes fell to the floor. The picture slides flew in every direction!

"I—I'm so sorry!" Flossie stammered as Mrs. Karilis helped her up. "I didn't mean to spill your pictures!" Her blue eyes filled with tears. "They're all mixed up now."

"Don't worry," Mr. Karilis assured her as Freddie and Bert hurried to pick up the slides. "It will be more fun not to know which picture is coming next!"

They all laughed and took seats. Mrs. Karilis turned out the lights and the show began.

"Most of these pictures were taken on the island of Crete," Mrs. Karilis explained. "It is in the Mediterranean south of the mainland of Greece. People were living on this island almost eight thousand years ago!"

"Those ruins sure look old," Bert observed as a picture flashed on the screen. It showed part of a wall built of stones and a roof supported by three dark red columns.

"This is the palace of Knossos," Mr. Karilis told them. "It was built for King Minos about three thousand years ago. Archaeologists discovered these ruins at the beginning of this century. Since then they have been uncovering as much of the old palace as they can. This next slide shows one of the pictures they found painted on a wall."

"The man's jumping over the bull!" Freddie cried excitedly. The picture showed a big bull. Holding onto the horns was one athlete while another stood behind the bull ready to catch the jumper.

"These are the famous 'bull dancers' of Crete," Mr. Karilis explained. "The king had young boys and girls brought from Athens and forced them to perform for him by vaulting over the bulls' horns."

"How dangerous!" Nan said with a shudder.

"I'd like to try it!" Freddie declared stoutly.

The next slide brought excited cries from all the children. It showed a large piece of stone standing on a barren hillside. "That's just like the drawing on the paper inside the fur hat!" Bert exclaimed. "The symbol of the bull's horns."

"That's right," Mr. Karilis agreed. "It is a sign one sees very often on Crete."

When Mr. Karilis had shown one box of slides, his wife said, "I think we've had enough pictures for one afternoon." She smiled at her young guests. "How would you like some of the baklava you rescued yesterday?"

When the children nodded eagerly, their hostess left the room and returned shortly with a pitcher of lemonade and a plate of the sugary cakes.

"These are yummy!" Flossie remarked as she finished the last crumb.

"Mm!" Freddie agreed. "I like Greek cakes."

The twins then thanked their hosts for the nice afternoon. "Please tell us if your brother finds the fur bale," Nan begged Mr. Karilis.

"I certainly will," he promised.

Back at home Bert and Nan went into the house to work a new puzzle. Freddie and Flossie wandered out into the back yard. "What could we play?" Flossie asked.

Freddie thought a minute. "I know!" he said. "Let's play bull jumpers."

"But how can we?" his twin cried. "We haven't any bull!"

At that moment Snap, the Bobbseys' large white shaggy dog bounded into the yard.

"There's our bull!" Freddie shouted. Snap stopped and looked at Freddie, his tail wagging vigorously.

"Snap doesn't have any horns!" Flossie said with a giggle.

Freddie looked discouraged. Then he started running toward the house.

"Where're you going?" Flossie called.

"I know where there are some horns!" Freddie disappeared inside.

A few minutes later the little boy was in the third-floor storage room, poking around in back of an old trunk. Suddenly the door opened and Dinah walked in.

"What're you doin', Freddie?" she asked suspiciously.

"I'm looking for those deer horns Daddy used to have on the wall in the den," the little boy said in a muffled voice as he lifted the lid of the trunk and peered in.

"What you want them for?"

"Flossie and I are going to play bull jumper," Freddie explained, "and I have to put the horns on Snap so he'll be a bull!"

"Snap's not goin' to like wearin' horns," Dinah warned with a chuckle. "But if you want to play with them they're over there." She pointed to a long shelf at the end of the room.

"Thanks, Dinah," Freddie said. He grabbed

the pair of deer's antlers and raced down the stairs.

Flossie was waiting. When she saw the antlers she clapped her hands. "Those are bee-yoo-ti-ful!" she exclaimed.

Freddie called Snap and set the antlers on the dog's head. Snap jerked about and the horns fell off.

"Oh, Snap!" moaned Flossie.

"How can we get them to stay on?" Freddie asked in disappointment.

"I know!" Flossie ran into the house and came back with a ball of string and a pair of scissors. She told Freddie to hold the antlers on Snap's collar. Then she wound the string around the horns and the leather collar until they held firm.

"There!" she said when she had finished. "They're not 'zactly in the right spot, but it's the only place to fasten them."

"They look neat!" Freddie cried in delight. Then he stood directly in front of Snap and grasped the antlers. "You stand back of him, Flossie, and catch me when I jump over just like they did in the picture."

Flossie hurried around back of Snap and took up her position. "Okay, bull jumper!" she called to Freddie, "I'm ready!"

CHAPTER III

YOUNG CHARIOT RACERS

"HERE I come!" Freddie cried. Putting his weight on the antlers, he prepared to jump over Snap's back.

At the pressure on his neck, the dog promptly lay down! "Snap!" Freddie protested, "you're supposed to be a fierce bull! Come on now! Get up!" He urged the dog to a standing position.

"Catch me, Flossie!" Freddie shouted, once more grasping the antlers.

But at that moment Snoop, the Bobbseys' black cat, walked by. He gave Snap a startled look. The cat's back arched, his black fur standing on end. Snoop's lip curled and he gave a loud hiss!

This was too much for Snap. He started for the cat. With a great leap Snoop landed on the trunk of the apple tree and raced up to a branch where he sat glaring down at the dog.

"I don't think Snap wants to be a bull!" Flossie observed sadly.

"Flossie!" Dinah called from the kitchen door. "You and Freddie come get ready for supper!"

Freddie reluctantly took the antlers off Snap's collar and the small twins ran into the house. Later, at the table, the four children gave an account of their visit to the Karilis home.

"How did you like the pictures of Greece?" Mr. Bobbsey asked.

"They were great!" Bert exclaimed. "We saw places that were thousands of years old!"

Flossie had been looking at her handsome father. He had a peculiar smile on his face.

"Daddy," she spoke up, "you have your s'prise look. What is it?"

Mr. Bobbsey threw back his head and laughed. "I can't ever fool my little fat fairy, can I?" he chuckled. "As a matter of fact, I do have a surprise for you!"

"Oh, goody!"

"Tell us, Dad!"

All the twins sat forward eagerly to hear their father's secret. With a wink at his wife, Mr. Bobbsey said, "How would you all like to go to Greece?"

"Go to Greece!" Nan echoed in astonishment. "Do you really mean it?"

"Yes, next week as soon as school is over," he replied with a big smile.

In answer to the children's excited questions, Mr. Bobbsey explained that he had been carrying on a correspondence for some time with a shipbuilder named Gorzako in Athens, Greece. They had been consulting about lumber to be used in building a new ship. Now Mr. Gorzako had invited Mr. Bobbsey to bring his family to Greece as his guests.

"How marvelous!" Nan cried.

"I can't wait!" squealed Flossie.

"We'll be able to work on the mystery of the stolen fur!" Bert exclaimed.

"Oh boy!" Freddie grinned.

"You children wouldn't be happy even in Greece if you didn't have a mystery to solve!" Mrs. Bobbsey said teasingly.

Freddie and Flossie jumped around the room, shouting, "We're going to Greece! We're going to Greece!"

"Mr. and Mrs. Gorzako have two children," their father went on, "a daughter Aliki, who is ten, and a son Mihalis, thirteen, so you'll have someone to play with."

"What funny names!" Flossie remarked.

"I imagine in English they would be Alice and Michael," her mother said, "but I think the Greek names sound very nice."

The twins began to beg their father for more details about the trip. He told them the family would leave the next Saturday and fly to Athens, arriving there on Sunday.

"The Gorzakos live on the beach near Athens," he continued. "I'm sure you children will enjoy yourselves."

"It sounds dreamy," Nan said with a sigh of delight.

Monday afternoon Nan met Flossie after school. "Bert is staying for baseball," she said. "How would you and Freddie like to go down to Mr. Karilis' shop? We can tell him about our trip to Greece."

"Freddie's gone home with Teddy Blake," Flossie said, "but I'll come with you."

The two girls set off for Lakeport center. Mr. Karilis was alone in the shop when they went in. "We're going to Greece!" Flossie cried as soon as she saw him.

"You are?" the fur man asked in surprise. "Tell me all about it!"

Nan quickly explained that they were going to visit Mr. and Mrs. Gorzako in Athens. When he had heard their plans Mr. Karilis beamed. "I'm sure you will like my country," he said. "I hope you will go to see my brother."

"We'd love to," Nan assured him. "Have the furs been found yet?"

He shook his head sadly. "I have not heard any more," he said. "And now I have another worry," he added. "Jim, my foreman, has left. He called up a little while ago and said he wouldn't be back!"

"That's too bad," Nan said sympathetically.

Mr. Karilis shrugged his shoulders. "I'll just have to look for another man." Then he smiled. "Now come into the workroom, girls. I have a feeling Flossie's dolls would like some new fur pieces!"

Flossie skipped along beside him happily. "My Linda never had a fur piece before. She'd love one," the little girl said.

Mr. Karilis picked up three small fur paws from a pile on a table. He handed them to a workman. In a few minutes the man gave them back. They had been sewed together to form a tiny fur scarf!

"Thank you," Flossie said, beaming. "Linda will be the most bee-yoo-ti-ful doll in the world!"

As they walked toward the door which led to the main room, Nan spotted a piece of paper on the floor by a desk. She picked it up. "Oh," she exclaimed, "this is another bull's horn!" She handed the paper to Mr. Karilis.

It was a torn bit of a letter, but half of the bull's horn symbol showed clearly. Mr. Karilis looked puzzled. "It must have fallen from Jim's desk," he guessed.

Nan picked up the piece of paper

"Jim said he didn't know anything about the bull's horn in the hat," Nan pointed out. "Why would he have this drawing?"

"It's all very strange," Mr. Karilis admitted. He picked up a card and wrote on it. "This is my brother's name and address," he said. "Perhaps you can find out something about the bull horns when you see him."

"We'll send you a letter," Flossie promised as the girls said good-by.

The next day in Bert and Nan's class their teacher, Miss Vandermeer, told the other boys and girls about the Bobbseys' trip. "Since Bert and Nan are going to Greece," she said, "I thought it would be interesting to tell you something about the ancient Greek games."

She explained that the early Greeks worshiped many gods and held athletic contests in their honor. "The Greeks were very athletic people," Miss Vandermeer said. "They loved to run, swim, wrestle, and race their chariots. The winner was crowned with a wreath of laurel leaves.

"The Olympic Games are the most famous," she continued. "They took place in Olympia, Greece, every four years for a long time and then were discontinued. But now they are held again in different cities all over the world."

The children nodded. They had heard of the Olympic Games.

Miss Vandermeer went on to tell about the Pythian Games held at Delphi and the Isthmian Games which took place near Corinth. "I hope Bert and Nan will be able to visit one of these places and tell us about it next year."

At that moment the bell rang, and the children ran out for recess. Bert's best friend, Charlie Mason, walked up to him. "Let's play some Greek games after school," he suggested.

"Say, that's a great idea!" Bert agreed.

Several other boys joined them, and soon they were busy making plans. Even Danny Rugg and Jack Westley said they would like to be in the foot race.

"How can we do the chariot race?" Dick Hatton, another classmate, asked.

Bert thought a minute. "We could use toy wagons for chariots and our dogs for horses," he suggested. "We'll run home and get them after school."

When Nan heard the plans she was interested. "There must have been some girls at the games," she said. "Can't Nellie and I do something?" Blond Nellie Parks was Nan's best friend.

"Well, Miss Vandermeer said the chariot races were started by the sound of trumpets," Bert replied. "You two be the trumpeters."

Freddie wanted to join the games too, so right after school he harnessed Waggo, the Bobbseys' frisky fox terrier, to his wagon and announced he would be in the chariot race. Bert whistled for Snap to be his horse.

Waggo jumped and wiggled so much that Freddie had a difficult time putting on his harness, but finally they were ready for the trip to school.

When they reached the building there was a crowd of boys and girls on the playground. The word that "Greek Games" were to be held had spread! Nan and Nellie were there with toy horns in their hands.

The first event was the foot race. Danny, Jack, Dick Hatton, Phil Moore, Charlie, and Bert lined up at the starting line. Nellie blew a blast on the "trumpet," and the boys were off.

"Come on, Bert!" Flossie called from the sidelines.

The race was very even. One minute Bert was ahead, then Charlie Mason. Danny Rugg was the last to start but gained steadily. Finally Bert, Charlie, and Danny were side by side approaching the finish line. Charlie managed an extra spurt of speed and dashed over the line followed closely by Danny, then Bert.

Nan was waiting there to declare the winner. "It's Charlie!" she cried. "He crossed the line first!"

Danny glowered at her, panting. "You just say that because you like Charlie," he blurted out. "I really won this race!"

Several other children were standing near Nan. They all agreed that Charlie was the winner. Danny looked sullen, but sauntered away as if he didn't care.

The chariot race was next. There were only four contestants, Charlie, Jack, Bert, and Freddie. They guided their dogs to the end of the field and took their places in the wagons. It took a few minutes to get the dogs to stand still, but finally Nan blew the starting signal. The charioteers sped off!

Cheering boys and girls lined the course. "Come on, Charlie!" they yelled. "Hurry up there, Jack!" "Attaboy, Bert!" "Ya-ay, Freddie!"

Waggo and Freddie were on the outside. The terrier frisked along at a fast pace. Then as Freddie passed Danny, who was standing on the sidelines, the bully held out his hand. Waggo jumped and grabbed at something.

The little wagon flipped over with a jerk, and Freddie was sent sprawling on the ground!

CHAPTER IV

THE PALACE OF PUZZLES

"FREDDIE!" cried Nan, dashing down the field to her little brother. "Are you hurt?"

"N-no, I'm okay, I guess." Freddie struggled to his feet. Just then he and Nan glanced at Waggo. He was swallowing the last of a string of hot dogs!

Nan whirled. "Danny Rugg!" she said angrily, "you made Waggo upset the wagon. You held out that meat as he came past!"

At this moment a cheer went up from the onlookers. Bert and Snap had won the chariot race!

The older Bobbsey boy jumped from his wagon and ran back to the little group. "What happened to Freddie?" he asked.

"Danny made Waggo upset his wagon," Nan explained.

Laughing loudly, the bully ran off to join Jack.

"That's too bad," Bert said. "Let's run the race over."

Freddie shook his head. "No, you won fair and square!"

Just then Nellie hurried up. She carried a crown made of green paper in her hand. "This is your laurel wreath, Bert," she said with a laugh. "It's as near as Nan and I could come to a real one." She placed the circle on Bert's head. He grinned sheepishly as the other boys and girls applauded.

The children were still talking about the "Greek Games" when school closed the following Thursday. Friday was a busy day with packing and last-minute errands. Early Saturday morning Sam drove the Bobbseys to the airport where the family boarded a plane for New York.

"Isn't this exciting!" Nan cried late that afternoon when she saw the huge jet plane which would fly them across the Atlantic.

"It certainly is," Mrs. Bobbsey agreed. "But you children must try to sleep right after we have our dinner on the plane. We reach Rome very early in the morning."

"Rome!" Freddie exclaimed. "I thought we were going to Athens!"

"We are, my little fat fireman," his father said, "but we refuel in Rome."

After a delicious meal the lights in the plane cabin were lowered and everyone settled down to sleep. The children felt their eyes had been closed only a few minutes when they were awakened by a voice over the loudspeaker.

"This is your captain speaking," it said. "We will reach the Rome airport in approximately fifteen minutes. The time on the ground is nine forty-five."

"That was an awful short sleep," Flossie complained.

"We've been going east toward the sun," her father told her, "so it's six hours later here than it is in New York."

After breakfast in the many-windowed restaurant of the air terminal the Bobbseys hurried back aboard and the jet took off for Athens. The children busied themselves with books and puzzles while Mrs. Bobbsey took out her knitting. It was late afternoon and the sun was low in the sky when the plane flew over the Greek city.

Mr. Bobbsey peered from the window and pointed out to the children a many-columned building which stood on a hill in the middle of Athens.

"That is the Parthenon," he explained. "It was built over two thousand years ago and is the most perfect example of its type of architecture in the world."

By this time the plane had left the city behind and was coming down onto the airfield. After a smooth landing the passengers filed out of the aircraft. As the Bobbsey family entered the terminal building, a smiling, dark-haired man approached them.

"I am Georgos," he introduced himself. "Mr. Gorzako has sent a car for you. I will help you with your luggage."

A short time later Georgos led the way from the building toward a Volkswagen bus. "Mr. Gorzako thought since there are six of you, you would be more comfortable in this," he said.

Freddie and Flossie giggled as they climbed into the high seats. "This is great!" Freddie declared.

After a fifteen-minute drive Georgos pulled up to a large white stucco house standing on a green lawn between the highway and a sandy beach. Mr. and Mrs. Gorzako welcomed the family heartily and introduced Aliki and Mihalis.

The girl was shorter than Nan, and her hair was darker. She smiled shyly at the Bobbseys. Mihalis, who was about Bert's height, had a very friendly manner. Both children spoke good English.

"See you tomorrow, Etsi," Mihalis called as the chauffeur drove away.

"I thought his name was Georgos," Bert remarked, surprised.

The Greek boy laughed. "It is, but he's always saying, *'Etsi-k'etsi,'* which means so-so, when anyone asks him how he is. So we call him Etsi."

"It's a good nickname," Bert agreed.

After dinner that evening the Gorzakos and the Bobbseys sat in the beautifully furnished living room. Nan noticed that on each table there was a string of beads. They were made of jade, amber, and other stones, and each one ended in a silken tassel.

"They're lovely!" she commented.

Mr. Gorzako picked up a string. "We call these worry beads," he said with a smile. "The Greek word for them is *komboloia*. They are very popular in this part of the world. I enjoy collecting them." He slowly fingered the beads, pushing them up and down on their cord.

"Why are they called worry beads?" Flossie asked curiously.

"When one's fingers are busy," Mr. Gorzako replied, "one has no time for worry."

The next morning Etsi brought the bus to the door. "I will take you to the Acropolis this morning," their host told the Bobbseys. "It is the most important thing to see in Athens."

During the drive Mr. Gorzako explained that

"acropolis" in ancient times really meant "fortification." Each settlement had its acropolis. "However," he went on, "the Athens Acropolis is the most famous because on it are the ruins of three buildings, the Parthenon, the Propylaea, and the Erectheion. You will see how beautiful they are."

A few minutes later Etsi parked the car, and the group began the climb to the Acropolis. As they passed through the entrance way, or Propylaea, Mr. Gorzako pointed out the marks of chariot wheels which could still be seen in the white rock.

"It's too bad Snap and Waggo aren't here with their chariots!" Flossie said with a giggle.

The Bobbseys followed their guide as he led them about the Acropolis explaining the different points of interest. The children were surprised to see the slabs of marble and broken pieces of columns which still littered the ground.

As the group walked toward the modern museum building some distance behind the Parthenon, Nan stopped to examine one of the honey-colored columns. "To think that this is over two thousand years old!" she mused to herself. She looked up just in time to see the others enter the museum.

"Help!" Flossie cried

"I must catch up with them!" Nan thought and began to run across the rock-strewn area. The next minute she sank to the ground with a little cry. Her foot had slipped between two large stones and she could not move!

Nan looked around desperately. At the moment there were no tourists near her. She struggled to pull her foot from the crack but it was caught tightly. She was about to call for help when she saw Flossie come out of the museum and look around.

Nan took a handkerchief from her skirt pocket and waved it frantically. Flossie spotted it and hurried toward her.

"Help me, Flossie!" Nan called. "I'm stuck!"

The little girl pushed and tugged at the big stones. They would not budge. Suddenly she saw two Greek boys a short distance away.

"Help!" Flossie cried. The boys ran over. It did not take them long to see what the trouble was.

By signs they made Nan understand that she was to pull her foot out when they moved one of the stones. The boys crouched side by side and gave the rock a great heave. It shifted just enough for Nan to release her foot, then it settled back again.

"Thank you!" Nan cried, rubbing her ankle.

The boys grinned and nodded, then ran off.

When the tour of the Acropolis was ended and the group was back in the bus, Bert told Mr. Gorzako about Mr. Karilis' brother Yannis. "Do you think we could stop at his factory?" the boy asked.

Their host agreed, and Etsi drove to the address on the card which Nan showed him. The four children went into the small building. Yannis Karilis proved to be shorter than his brother but had the same friendly smile.

In reply to Bert's question, he said that the police had not yet found Thanos or the bale of fur.

"What does Thanos look like?" Nan asked.

"Well, like most Greeks, he has dark hair and eyes. He is short and rather plump," Yannis said.

"Isn't there *anything* different about him?" Bert persisted.

Yannis Karilis thought a moment, then told him that the workman had unusually thick eyebrows which came together across his nose. "Thanos came from Crete," he continued. "Perhaps he has gone back there."

The twins said good-by to the fur man and promised to come and see him again while they were in Athens. As they left, a bright-eyed boy of about eight hurried to open the door for them.

"Kali andamosi," he said politely.

"That must be Greek for good-by," Nan guessed. "We ought to learn how to answer him."

Back in the car on the way to the house, Bert asked Mr. Gorzako to teach them a few words of Greek.

He gladly agreed. "The two most useful words in any language," he began, "are 'please' and 'thank you.' In Greek, *parakalo* means 'please' and *efcharisto* means 'thank you.'"

"Efcharisto for telling us!" Flossie cried.

"And did you know that our country is divided into 'dry Greece' and 'wet Greece'?" Mr. Gorzako asked with a smile. In answer to the children's questions, he explained that the mainland was called "dry Greece" while the many islands in the seas around it were "wet Greece."

"Crete is one of the oldest and most interesting islands," he continued. "Would you like to see it?"

"Oh, yes!" Nan exclaimed. "And maybe we could look for Thanos."

It was decided that the Bobbseys would fly to Crete the next morning. Mr. Gorzako arranged for a guide and car to meet them on the island and take them to see the ruins of the ancient palace of Knossos.

"Don't pick up any old statues or bits of

ruins," Mr. Gorzako said teasingly to the twins at the airport. "They all belong to the government, and it's against the law to take them out of the country without a permit."

"If *I* find anything I'll give it to the President," Flossie assured him solemnly.

Mr. Gorzako laughed. "You'll have to give it to the king!" he replied. "We don't have a president in Greece."

When the Bobbseys arrived on Crete the guide, who introduced himself as Sofoklis, drove them directly to the ruins of the palace of Knossos. The children were excited at being in the place they had seen in Mr. Karilis' slides.

As they followed Sofoklis down a broad stone staircase and into room after room, Freddie was wide-eyed. "This would be a neat place to play hide and seek!"

"Do you know the legend of the labyrinth?" the guide asked.

"No, tell us!" the children begged, and Flossie added, "What's a labrinth?"

Sofoklis smiled. "A labyrinth," he said, "is a kind of puzzle or maze."

The guide then explained that King Minos had caused his palace to be built with such a network of rooms and passageways that once a person became lost, it was impossible for him to find his way out.

"And in the farthest room of this labyrinth," he went on, "lived the Minotaur, a monster half human and half bull. When Theseus, the King of Athens' handsome son, came to Crete he vowed to slay the Minotaur."

"Ooh!" Flossie cried, her eyes wide.

"But Ariadne, the daughter of King Minos, fell in love with Theseus and gave him a ball of string to unwind as he went into the labyrinth. And so, after Theseus had killed the monster, he was able to find his way out again!"

"That's a wonderful story," Nan remarked as they continued their way through the underground ruins.

In one room, which Sofoklis told them had been the apartment of the queen, Flossie was fascinated by a painting on one wall. She walked closer to examine it. Against a grayish background many happy-looking blue fish seemed to be playing. There were also tiny fish, some painted pink and some yellow.

Flossie smiled as she gazed at the picture. "I'd like to have that in my room at home," she thought. A little later she looked around. The others had disappeared.

Flossie ran out of the room and down a corridor. She turned several corners, then stopped suddenly.

"I'm—I'm lost!" Flossie wailed.

CHAPTER V

A STRANGE PACKAGE

THE little lost girl looked up and down the corridor, wondering what to do. "I'll go back to the fish picture," Flossie decided.

She turned around and started down the hall. But it did not lead back to the queen's apartment. Flossie made a few turns and then stopped, hopelessly confused.

"Mommy! Daddy!" she called tearfully. There was no reply.

Meanwhile, the other Bobbseys had entered what the guide told them had been the ancient throne room. It had been restored to show what it had looked like in the days of King Minos. The walls were a soft red. In the center of one there was a high-backed stone seat.

"This is the throne," Sofoklis told them. "It is the oldest one in Europe."

Mrs. Bobbsey glanced around at the children. "Where's Flossie?" she exclaimed anxiously.

At that moment they heard the little girl's faint cry. "Go get her, please, Bert," his mother said with concern. "She doesn't know where we are."

Bert ran from the room, but soon returned. "I can hear Flossie, but I can't find her," he reported. "She's lost in the labyrinth!"

"If you only had Ariadne's string," Nan said, "everything would be all right."

Mrs. Bobbsey rummaged in her big handbag and pulled out the knitting she had started on the plane coming to Athens. She handed the ball of yarn to Bert.

"Here you are, Theseus," she said with a smile. "Use this."

Bert took the yarn and started off. He called Flossie at intervals and tried to follow the sound of her voice when she answered. But the stone walls made an echo. At times her calls seemed nearby and then they would fade away. As he went, Bert unwound the yarn. In a few minutes the ball was almost gone and he had still not reached his little sister.

"Don't move, Flossie!" he called. "Stay right where you are so I can find you." A few seconds later he heard a sob. He turned a corner. There, huddled at the foot of a large stone pillar, was Flossie!

When the little girl saw her brother she

jumped up and threw her arms around him. "Oh, Bert!" she cried, "thank you for finding me. I thought I was lost forever!"

"We wouldn't let anything like that happen to you, Floss," said Bert, giving her a hug.

With Flossie clinging to his belt, Bert retraced his steps, following the trail of yarn and winding it onto the ball as he walked.

When Bert and Flossie reached the throne room everyone cried out in relief.

"Ariadne's trick still works," Nan said happily. "You found your way out of the labyrinth!"

Later, after the ruins of the palace had been thoroughly explored, the group turned toward the entrance gate. As they walked along, the guide called their attention to several huge pits lined with large stones. At the bottom of one could be seen part of a flight of steps.

"In the days of King Minos," Sofoklis explained, "pottery that became broken and useless was thrown into these holes."

The children peered down into the deep pit. "Look," Nan said. "There's a package." She pointed to an object close to the bottom of one wall.

"Let me get it!" Freddie volunteered. "Somebody hold me, okay?"

But the pit was far too deep to do this. The

guide ran over to the gatekeeper's lodge and came back with a rope ladder.

"I think this will just reach to the top of those remaining five steps," Sofoklis said, as he lowered the ladder. The guide had guessed correctly. While he and Mr. Bobbsey held the rope ladder steady, Freddie climbed down it and onto the stone steps. In a few minutes he was up again, with the package tucked into the front of his shirt.

"It feels sort of heavy," the little boy said as he put the bundle down on the ground. Quickly he tore off the old handkerchief in which it was wrapped.

"It's a chariot!" Flossie cried in surprise. She picked up a tiny bronze chariot drawn by two little bronze horses. There were flecks of dirt clinging to it.

"This will be great to play with!" Freddie said enthusiastically.

"You can't keep it, Freddie!" Flossie reminded him. "We promised Mr. Gorzako we'd give all the statues we found to the king!"

Mr. Bobbsey laughed. "I think it would be all right to turn it in to the head of the museum in town," he said. Sofoklis agreed.

When they reached the museum they found a Mr. Telides in charge. He examined the little chariot which Freddie handed to him.

In a few minutes Freddie was up again

"This looks as if it may have come from the palace ruins," he said slowly, "but I'll have our expert look at it. In the meantime would you like to see our museum?"

"Parakalo!" Freddie said, grinning.

Mr. Telides led the group through the beautiful building. He showed them the original paintings of the bull jumpers which had been taken from the walls of the ancient palace. He also pointed out a tiny statue of an acrobat.

"I think he's jumping over a bull!" Flossie declared as she peered at the little figure.

"He has only one leg!" Freddie cried.

"We think he is a bull jumper," the museum director said with a smile, "but he didn't lose his leg that way. It's because he's been around for over three thousand years!"

Nan had walked into the next room where there were many glass cases of small objects.

"These things were found by workers digging in the ruins of the palace of Knossos," Mr. Telides said as he led the others into the room.

Nan leaned closer to see the little figures of horses, bulls, and goats in one case. "There's a chariot like the one we found!" she cried.

The director nodded. "Yes, it is similar," he agreed. "Our expert will make sure. If you would like to have your lunch, his report will be ready by the time you come back here."

Mr. and Mrs. Bobbsey agreed to the idea. They thanked Mr. Telides, and the guide took them to a restaurant on the town square.

They were greeted by the proprietor, a big man with curly black hair. *"Kalos ilthate!"* he boomed. Proudly he added, "I speak English. I said 'welcome'!"

He ushered the group to a table. Then he pointed to the kitchen and said, "Please step in there and see what the cook has made. We will serve you whatever you think looks good!"

"This is fun!" Flossie remarked as she looked about the kitchen. The cook raised a lid to let her sniff the contents of a pot.

Everything smelled so good the children could not make up their minds. Finally the cook led them over to a large pan which contained some crusty, spicy-smelling food.

"This is *moussaka*," he said. "It is a very popular dish in Greece. Why don't you try it?"

They all decided to have some. When the waiter brought the heaped-up plates to the table, Mrs. Bobbsey tasted the moussaka. "It's delicious," she declared. "It seems to be ground beef with eggplant and cheese."

When the waiter brought plates of ripe strawberries for dessert, Bert had an idea. "Remember Yannis Karilis said his workman Thanos came from Crete," he said. "Maybe he's hiding out somewhere around here."

But when Bert asked the waiter if he knew a man named Thanos who had been working in an Athens fur factory, the man shook his head.

"Are there any fur factories in Crete?" Nan persisted.

"There is one at the edge of town," the waiter replied. "It was closed for some time, but I believe they've started working again in the past few weeks."

"Let's go to the factory," Bert proposed. "Someone there may have heard of Thanos."

The waiter gave Sofoklis directions how to reach the place and the group drove off. They found the factory in the oldest part of the town. It stood at the corner of two narrow streets.

The children piled out of the car. Sofoklis followed. They found a door of the factory standing partway open. As Bert and Flossie started in, a man barred their way. He was rather plump with black bushy eyebrows which met over his nose.

"Oh!" cried Flossie excitedly. "You're Thanos!"

CHAPTER VI

A SUSPECT ESCAPES

THE plump man glared at Flossie. *"Then katalamvano!"* he muttered.

"He says he doesn't understand," explained Sofoklis, who was right behind Bert and Flossie. "I'll ask him what his name is." He turned to the man at the door and spoke in Greek.

But before the guide could finish, the black-eyebrowed man slammed the door in their faces!

"What was that all about?" Mr. Bobbsey asked when the children walked back to the car.

Bert explained. "I don't know—I'm *sure* that man was Thanos," he declared. "Maybe we'd better report him to the police."

"You're right, son," Mr. Bobbsey agreed and directed Sofoklis to drive to police headquarters.

When they reached it they met the friendly

officer in charge. He spoke English and listened carefully as Bert explained about the theft of Mr. Karilis' fur and their search for Thanos.

"I'll send two English-speaking men from our department out there with you," said the officer. "They can find out what's going on in that factory."

The police followed the Bobbsey car out to the old building. This time when they walked up to the entrance the door was closed. One of the policemen knocked loudly. There was no reply. He knocked again. After several minutes the door opened.

A thin man with a black mustache stood there. He was wearing tight trousers and a sleeveless jacket over a white shirt. A dark red sash was wound around his waist.

There followed a long conversation in Greek between the man and the policemen. Finally the officer turned to the children. "This man is the manager. His name is Dimitris. He says he knows nothing about a man called Thanos."

"Can't we go in and look around?" Nan suggested. "My brother and sister are sure the man they saw is the one we're looking for."

The policeman turned to Dimitris and asked another question. The man glared at Nan, then shrugged his shoulders and stood aside to allow the children and the police to enter.

They walked into a large room, filled with several long tables. Men seated at them were working busily, cutting and sewing narrow strips of fur. Bert peered at each one carefully. The man who had come to the door the first time was not in the room.

When Bert reached the end of the second table he noticed Dimitris glancing nervously out the front entrance. "I wonder what he's worried about," Bert thought.

The boy sauntered toward the door, looked up and down the main street, then stepped out into the sunshine. Mr. and Mrs. Bobbsey were sitting in the car chatting with Sofoklis.

Bert walked down the street which ran along the side of the factory. As he rounded the corner, a door at the back of the building opened slowly and a man hurried out.

"That's Thanos!" Bert cried aloud. He began to run down the street toward the man.

When the man heard the boy's footsteps on the stone pavement he looked back, startled. Then he turned and dashed off down the road. Bert raced after him.

Although the man was plump he was quick. Bert had all he could do to keep him in sight as he dodged around corners and down the narrow streets.

"Stop!" Bert called, but the fugitive paid no attention.

The next minute the man darted past an intersection, then retraced his steps and ran up an unpaved side street. At the same moment a man led a donkey around the same corner. The little animal was laden with brightly colored jugs and dishes. They were piled so high that all that could be seen of him was his long face, pointed ears, and little spindly legs.

Bert was moving too fast to stop. *Crash!* He ran into the donkey. The force of the collision broke the cord which held the pottery. The dishes scattered in all directions!

The donkey man began to shout and wave his arms. Bert tried to think of a Greek phrase. Finally he stammered, *"Signomi."* He had heard Sofoklis use this word and decided it meant "excuse me."

The man stopped yelling and smiled at Bert. He put one arm around the boy's shoulders and with the other indicated that together they would pick up the pottery.

When the dishes and jugs were all once more fastened onto the donkey's back, the man shook Bert's hand warmly and continued on his way. The boy looked around. The bushy-browed man he had been chasing had disappeared.

"I'll never be able to find him now," Bert told himself. He turned and walked back to the fur factory. The other children and the policemen were waiting for him.

The dishes scattered in all directions

"Where have you been?" Nan asked.

Bert told about seeing the plump, dark-haired man leave the building by the other door. "I chased him," the boy explained, "but he got away."

"Then Dimitris was not telling the truth," the policeman said, "when he told us there was no such man in the factory. We'll keep watch over this place and try to pick up the person you think is a thief."

After thanking the policemen, Sofoklis and the Bobbseys drove back to the museum. There Mr. Telides welcomed them with a smile. "I have a report on the bronze chariot you found," he announced.

"Is it a real old one?" Freddie asked eagerly.

"Yes, it is," the director said, "and we're very glad to add it to our exhibits. We are grateful to you for bringing it to us. If we only knew exactly where it had been dug up, we could go there and perhaps locate more valuable articles."

"Let's go back to the king's palace," Flossie pleaded with her father. "Maybe we can find another chariot!"

"At least we might be able to discover more about this one," Bert put in. "Please, Dad, let's go!"

Mr. Bobbsey looked at his watch. "We have two hours before our plane leaves for Athens," he said. "That will give you about an hour out at the palace of Knossos. Sofoklis can take you children and pick up your mother and me on the way to the airfield."

"Thank you, Dad!" the twins cried and ran out to the car.

When they arrived at the palace ruins once more, Sofoklis found a man he knew who was a guard there. The guard spoke English, so Bert explained about finding the wrapped-up bronze chariot in the pit. The guard was amazed.

"Have you seen anyone digging around here?" Nan asked him. "Mr. Telides at the museum thought if we could locate the place where the chariot was found, there might be other things too."

"No one digs here without a permit from the government," the guard replied sternly.

"But couldn't someone have sneaked in and done some digging even though he wasn't s'posed to?" Freddie suggested.

The guard thought a minute. "As a matter of fact," he began slowly, "yesterday I saw a man way over there by that stone wall. He looked as if he was digging so I walked over. He had a shovel, but when I questioned him he said he didn't know it was against the law to dig. Anyway, he said he hadn't found anything. I ordered him to leave the grounds at once."

"Did you see him leave?" Bert asked.

The guard replied that he had been called to another part of the grounds at that moment. "I asked the gatekeeper later about the man. He told me the stranger had left in a great hurry."

"Maybe the man wrapped the chariot in his handkerchief and dropped it into that hole because he was afraid you'd find it," Freddie said to the guard.

"And maybe he thought he'd come back later and get it!" Flossie added.

"Only Nan found the chariot first," Bert said.

"What did the stranger look like?" Nan asked curiously.

"He was Greek—thin, with a black mustache," the guard replied.

The twins wished they might look around some more, but Sofoklis spoke up. "We must get back to town. It is time to catch the plane."

The children were sorry to leave. The guard assured them, however, he would tell the museum director about the man with the shovel and show him where the chariot probably had been found.

All the conversation during the hour's flight back to Athens was about the exciting discovery of the bronze chariot and the man the children were sure was Thanos. Etsi met them at the airport and drove them to the Gorzako home.

Mr. Gorzako was astonished when Flossie told him about finding the ancient little chariot. "I hope the police on Crete will be able to catch the man who dug it up," he said. "He may be part of that group suspected of smuggling relics out of Greece."

"I wish we could have stayed to help the policemen," Freddie declared wistfully.

"Well, at least you've given them some good clues to work on," Mr. Gorzako said. "Perhaps if you Bobbseys had come to Greece sooner, we wouldn't have lost so many of our valuable treasures," he added with a smile.

After dinner Nan said to Bert, "Don't you think we should tell Mr. Yannis Karilis about seeing the man we think was Thanos?"

"Sure thing, Sis," her twin replied. "We'll call him first thing tomorrow."

After breakfast the next morning Bert called the fur factory and reported their adventures of the previous day.

"That's very interesting," Yannis declared. "Thanos came from Crete. He may very likely have gone back there to hide out. I'm glad you put the police on his trail."

"We'll keep looking for him," Bert assured the fur man before hanging up.

Since the visit to Crete had been rather strenuous, Mrs. Gorzako suggested that the Bobbseys spend the day on the beach. All gladly agreed to the plan.

The twins, with Aliki and Mihalis, spent most of the time happily swimming in the calm water and playing in the sand.

Late in the afternoon Mr. Gorzako found Flossie in the living room standing beside a table. She was fingering the string of jade beads which lay there.

"And what are you doing with my worry beads?" he asked teasingly.

Flossie sighed. "I'm worried," she replied. "I'm afraid Thanos has gone off with Mr. Karilis' furs and we won't be able to get them back."

Early the next day the telephone rang. It was Yannis calling Bert. "Don't try to find Thanos," the fur man cried when the boy answered.

"Why not?" Bert asked, bewildered.

"It's too dangerous! I have received a warning!"

CHAPTER VII

GREEK HOPSCOTCH

"A warning!" Bert repeated. "What do you mean, sir?"

"I've just received a post card through the mail," Yannis Karilis explained. "It says to 'Keep the American children out of my business or there will be trouble. You mustn't try to find Thanos. You might be hurt.' "

"Where was the card mailed?" Bert asked.

The fur man replied that the card was postmarked Athens. "However, the picture on it is a scene on Crete," he added.

"Crete!" Bert exclaimed. "Then the man I chased on Tuesday *was* Thanos. He probably went to Crete and came back to Athens."

"It is very possible," Yannis agreed. "He knows the fur came from my brother in America, so he decided you were helping me try to find him."

When Bert reported this conversation to the rest of the Bobbseys, his mother looked worried.

60

"Perhaps you had better forget about Mr. Karilis' stolen fur." she said. "Thanos may be a dangerous man."

"We'll be careful, Mother," Nan promised. "But Yannis needs the fur so his people will have work."

Mrs. Bobbsey hugged her daughter. "I know you want to be helpful, dear, but please don't take any chances."

At that moment Aliki came into the room. She told the twins that she and Mihalis had invited some of their English-speaking friends to come over that afternoon to meet their American guests.

"We'll have fun," she said happily. "We can play games."

Shortly after lunch four Greek children arrived. There were two little girls about eight and two boys, one ten and the other thirteen. After they had all been introduced, Aliki and Mihalis led them out onto a stone terrace overlooking the beach.

"What shall we play first?" Aliki asked.

One of the girls, whose name was Sofia, spoke up. "Let's play *koutso!*" she proposed.

"Do you know how, Nan?" Mihalis asked.

Nan shook her head doubtfully. "I don't think so," she replied.

"We'll teach you!" Aliki assured her. The Greek girl ran into the house and returned with a piece of chalk. She drew a big rectangle on the stone floor and then marked it off into ten spaces.

Flossie whispered to Freddie, "It looks like hopscotch."

"Mother says the game *koutso* came from Crete," Aliki informed the Americans. "It's supposed to be the maze that Theseus went through to kill the Minotaur."

"Oh, the labyrinth!" Nan cried. "Then Bert played koutso the other day," she added with a laugh, "when he rescued Flossie."

When the Greek children explained how to play, Bert nodded. "We know the game. It's called hopscotch where we live."

It was a lively contest, and finally Flossie was declared the winner. "Now you choose the next game," Aliki urged her.

"Let's play tag," Flossie proposed.

The Greek children nodded. "Yes, we know that one," the other little girl, named Daphni, said. Then she began to count, *"Am, stra, dam; pica, pica, rum."* She ended with her finger pointed at Freddie.

"She was counting out," Flossie said with a giggle, "and Freddie, you're It."

"Just as we say eeny, meeny, miney, mo," Nan remarked.

Freddie dashed about trying to catch one of the children. Finally Bert stumbled, and Freddie tagged him. There were many shrieks and giggles as Bert chased the others around the terrace and out onto the lawn.

After tag, one of the boys suggested playing "statues." "Do you know how?" he asked Bert.

"Sure! We play statues too!"

"Isn't it nice," Aliki remarked, "that we have the same games in Greece and America?"

Mihalis was chosen to be sculptor. He spun the smaller children very carefully. As he let go, each child froze into position.

Flossie sat down hard, her legs stretched out in front of her. Nan kept her balance on one foot with her arms flung into the air. Grinning, Mihalis swung Bert particularly hard. The Bobbsey boy turned a somersault and landed squarely on his two feet.

"You're all good," Mihalis said as he looked around at the "statues" on the lawn. "But I think Freddie wins. He's the Discus Thrower!"

Freddie had landed in the position of the famous Greek statue. He was bent over with his weight on his right foot, his right arm raised behind him and his left hand on his right knee.

All the Greek children clapped their hands, and Freddie grinned proudly. Then Mrs. Grozako came out onto the terrace with a tray of fruit juice and cakes. The children chattered happily as they enjoyed their refreshments.

That evening after Mr. Gorzako had heard about the party, he said thoughtfully, "You've seen a part of 'wet Greece' in Crete. How would you like to see something of 'dry Greece'?"

"That would be great!" Bert spoke up.

Mr. Gorzako explained that since he and his wife could not accompany them, he would have Etsi drive the Bobbseys to some of the famous archaeological spots. "You will be able to see the ruins of ancient Greek cities which have been uncovered in the past hundred years," he said. "Delphi and Corinth are two of the most interesting."

Then, noticing that Mihalis and Aliki looked sad at the thought of their guests leaving for a few days, he asked his children, "Would you like to go along?"

"Oh, yes," they both cried happily.

It was arranged that Mr. and Mrs. Bobbsey, the twins and the Gorzako children would leave the next morning in the Volkswagen bus.

That night as they were getting ready for bed, Bert said to Freddie, "What's the matter? You look glum, chum. Don't you want to go on the trip?"

"I think we should stay here and look for Thanos," Freddie said seriously.

"We won't be gone very long," Bert assured his brother. "Anyway, the police are looking for Thanos."

As Freddie brightened a little, Bert added, "Something exciting is bound to happen on the trip. It always does when we travel!"

"That's right," Freddie replied more cheerfully. "And maybe we can find some more chariots!"

It was a bright sunny morning when Etsi loaded the luggage and his passengers into the little bus. They drove along the sea for a while, then through the city of Athens and out into the country on the other side. Here entire families were working in fertile fields.

"Most of Greece is mountainous," Etsi explained, "so we have to grow our food wherever we find a bit of level land. This section produces the majority of our vegetables."

As the Bobbseys peered from the bus they saw tiny children stumbling along the furrows lugging great baskets in their arms. The women all wore white cloths tied over their heads.

"The scarfs protect them from the hot sun," Aliki pointed out. "And see, in the country the children work as hard as their parents."

Late in the morning Etsi drew up beneath the shade of a huge olive tree which grew along the side of the road. He reached into a compartment and took out thermos bottles and a white box.

"That looks like the box of baklava we found in Lakeport!" Nan observed with a smile.

"It is baklava," Etsi replied. "Mrs. Gorzako

thought you might be hungry before we reached Delphi so she sent along some juice and cakes."

"We can eat under the tree," Aliki proposed, opening the door and jumping out.

The others followed. Etsi poured the juice into plastic cups and everyone stood under the old tree sipping their drinks and munching on the baklava. A soft breeze sprang up and ruffled the girls' hair.

Suddenly Flossie pointed ahead. A little donkey was trotting toward them. A big basket of green fodder hung from each side of his saddle. A girl about Nan's age was leading the animal. Both the girl and the donkey wore strings of blue beads around their necks!

"I never saw a donkey with beads before!" Flossie giggled.

"Most Greek children and animals in the country wear blue beads," Etsi told her. "They're supposed to protect them from the 'evil eye' or anything which would do them harm."

"Kalimera!" Mihalis called out to the girl.

"He said, 'Good morning,' " Aliki explained to the twins.

"Kalimera," the country girl replied shyly.

"Maybe she'd like a cake," Nan said and held out the box with a smile.

The girl halted the donkey and walked timidly over to Nan. She took a piece of the baklava and tasted it. A look of delight came over her face.

"Efcharisto!" she said softly.

Nan fingered a string of yellow beads which hung around her neck. "I wonder if she'd trade?" she asked Aliki.

"I'll ask her," Aliki volunteered. She turned to the country girl and asked a question in Greek. She pointed to Nan's yellow beads.

The country girl's eyes widened and she shook her head violently. She spoke rapidly. Then she ran back to her donkey and urged him on down the road. When she was a safe distance away she turned and waved to the group under the tree.

"I guess she didn't want to trade," Nan remarked sadly.

Aliki laughed. "No, she said yellow beads wouldn't work the same way the blue ones do. She would be afraid to exchange them for yours."

Etsi suggested that they should be on their way if they wished to reach Delphi in time for lunch. The bus went on through the countryside and presently began climbing as the road wound up into the mountains.

The Bobbseys peered out at the huge masses of rock sparsely covered with clumps of grass and low bushes. Here and there goats or sheep could be spotted grazing on the steep slopes.

The road seemed to cling to the side of the mountains as the bus made its way higher and higher. Suddenly the group found themselves

She took a piece of the baklava

riding along a narrow street between high stone houses. In front of each house brightly colored bags, blouses, and skirts were hung on lines.

"This is the village of Arakhova," Etsi said. "It is famous for its woven articles."

Mrs. Bobbsey and Nan gazed longingly at the brilliant clothes as Etsi drove through the town without stopping. Once out of the village the road began a gradual descent. Far down to one side could be seen what looked almost like a green sea.

"Those are olive trees," Etsi said. "It's the finest and oldest grove in Greece."

"It's a long way down there!" Nan said with a little shiver as she glanced over the cliff.

At that moment they rounded a corner. The ground to the left of the road here sloped down a little more moderately.

"Say!" Bert cried. "Look at those tire tracks! A car must have gone over the edge!"

In the soft ground between the pavement and the slope could be seen heavy tire markings. Etsi quickly pulled over and stopped the bus. Mr. Bobbsey and the boys jumped out and ran across the road.

"There it is!" Bert exclaimed. He pointed down the steep slope. About twenty yards below where they stood, they saw a truck smashed against a huge boulder!

CHAPTER VIII

THE MYSTERY TRUCK

"LET'S see if anyone's in the truck!" Mihalis cried, beginning to scramble down the steep incline. Bert followed.

"Be careful!" Mr. Bobbsey called as he and Etsi picked their way after the boys.

When the four reached the vehicle they saw that it had run headlong into the rock. The radiator was smashed in. There was no sign of anybody in the cab.

"That's strange," Mr. Bobbsey declared. "The driver must have jumped clear before the truck hit the boulder."

"I wonder if there's anything in the back," Bert said. The rear door of the closed truck had been sprung open by the crash. The boy boosted himself up and looked around the inside of the truck.

There was a bit of blue paper on the floor which he stuffed into his pocket. Otherwise the truck seemed to be empty. Then, just as he was preparing to jump out, Bert spotted something dark by the door. He stooped and picked it up. It felt soft in his hand. He leaped to the ground and opened his fingers.

He had picked up a little bunch of fur paws!

"That's odd!" Bert exclaimed. "The truck must have been carrying furs. But where are they?"

Mihalis had been examining the side of the truck. Now he pointed to one of the front doors. "Look," he said. "The name's been painted out!"

"You're right!" Bert cried. "I can barely make out a K at the beginning and this queer zigzag at the end!"

"That zig-zag is the Greek S," Mihalis informed him with a grin.

"The name begins with a K and ends in S," Bert said thoughtfully. "I wonder if this could possibly be the truck Thanos stole from Mr. Karilis!"

"Say!" Mihalis said admiringly. "Maybe it is. You're a great detective, Bert!"

Mr. Bobbsey and Etsi had climbed back to the road to report to Mrs. Bobbsey, Freddie, and the girls. The two boys hurried after them.

When Bert showed the others the fur paws

"Look," he said. "The name's been painted out."

and told them about the painted-out name, Nan was excited. "Maybe the driver was Thanos!" she cried. "He could be around here some place!"

"If he is, we'll find him!" Freddie assured her stoutly as Etsi headed toward Delphi once more.

A few minutes later the car rounded a curve. Before them two mountains of rock soared toward the blue sky. The peaks were separated by a deep cleft. Near the bottom of the cleft several marble columns could be seen.

"Those are the ruins of the sanctuary of Delphi," Etsi told them.

"How beautiful!" Nan said softly as she gazed at the impressive view.

"We'll come back late this afternoon with a guide," Mihalis explained. "The sun is too hot for sightseeing in the middle of the day."

By this time they had driven past the ruins and into the little town of Delphi. Its main street was lined with hotels and shops. Etsi drew up before one of the hotels and stopped.

"Mr. Gorzako made reservations for us here," he remarked.

While Mr. Bobbsey was registering, Bert began talking with the man behind the desk. "Was anyone hurt in that truck accident?" the boy asked.

The clerk looked puzzled. "What accident?"

When Bert described the smashed truck which they had seen, the clerk picked up the phone and called the police. After a brief conversation he turned back to Bert. "The police did not know of this," he said. "They will have the truck hauled into a garage, and try to find out what happened to the driver."

Mrs. Bobbsey then told the children all their rooms were on the second floor.

"Come on, Freddie," Flossie said, "let's run up!" The small twins started toward a broad stairway nearby.

"No, no," a hotel porter called after them. "One goes *down* to the second floor! You take the elevator. I bring bags later."

The Bobbsey family, with Aliki and Mihalis, stepped into the elevator and Mr. Bobbsey pushed the button marked "2." The elevator began to move. "We *are* going down!" Nan cried in astonishment as the "6" lighted up, then the "5" and so on until at "2" the car stopped and the door rolled open.

When they walked into their rooms the explanation was clear. The hotel was built into the side of the mountain and the room floors went down from the street level rather than up.

Hands and faces were quickly washed, and the party met on the outdoor terrace overlooking a deep gorge. Far below could be seen the olive grove and in the distance a bit of blue sea.

"Isn't it bee-yoo-ti-ful!" Flossie cried as she sat down at the luncheon table. The others agreed.

After lunch, Etsi brought the bus around again and drove them up to the sanctuary. Their guide was waiting. He was tall and thin with merry brown eyes. He introduced himself as Alexandros.

"First, let me tell you that you are on Mount Parnassus, the home of the ancient gods of Greek mythology," Alexandros said. "Apollo, who was the god of Light and Music, swam over here from Crete disguised as a dolphin and took Delphi under his protection."

While the children listened entranced, he told them that almost three thousand years ago, Delphi had been the seat of the most famous oracle in the Greek world. Important people came to Delphi from great distances to ask the oracle what to do. As a result, many temples and shrines were erected in the area. A stadium was built where the Pythian games took place, and a theater where plays were given.

"I wish there were mythological gods here now," Nan said dreamily. "I'd like to see Apollo."

Alexandros smiled. "Some people think the

gods are still with us," he said mysteriously.

"Where are they?" Freddie cried excitedly.

"Have you ever heard of Pan?" Alexandros asked.

"Yes." Bert spoke up. "He has goat's horns and hoofs, and plays on a pipe!"

"That's right," Alexandros agreed. "I see you have studied some Greek mythology. Pan is the god of the goatherds, and some of them say he still lives in one of the many caves on Parnassus. They have heard him playing his pipes at night!"

"That's neat!" Bert exclaimed.

"My nephew Petros is a goatherd in the summer," Alexandros remarked. "He spends the nights on the mountain with his goats. He has heard the pipes."

"I wish I could sleep in the mountains," Freddie said eagerly. "Maybe I'd see Pan!"

"Why not?" Alexandros queried with a smile. "Petros would be glad to have company in his hut."

"Could we, Daddy?" Freddie asked, his blue eyes blazing with excitement.

Mr. and Mrs. Bobbsey held a consultation with the guide. It was finally decided that Bert, Freddie, and Mihalis could spend the night with Petros on the mountain.

"Wow!" Freddie shouted. "Let's go!"

Etsi drove the party back to town where Bert and Mihalis bought food to take along for their supper. Then he took the boys and Alexandros in the bus as far up the mountain as the road ran. Etsi bade the four good-by, and they set off on foot, with the guide leading the way.

The narrow path wound in and out among rocks and small clumps of bushes. Wild thyme spread over the mountainside. Here and there tall cypress trees dotted the landscape. In the distance they could hear the tinkle of bells. Alexandros explained that these were fastened to the goats' necks so that if they happened to stray, the animals could be found.

Finally when the group had climbed for almost half an hour, they saw a crude shack ahead of them. It was made of brush, with a thatched roof, and had only three sides.

A thin, dark-haired boy about Bert's age came to meet them. He carried a staff topped by a curved handle.

"Petros!" Alexandros called. "I have guests for you!" He then began speaking in Greek.

The boy listened with a smile. He came forward and solemnly shook hands with Mihalis, Bert, and Freddie. He motioned toward his hut. "Kalos ilthate," he said.

Bert remembered this meant "welcome." "Efcharisto," he replied with a grin.

Alexandros waved good-by to the boys and told them it would be an easy walk down to the village in the morning. When he had disappeared around a bend in the path, Mihalis showed Petros the package of food they had brought. The young goatherd beamed.

"Let's have supper," Freddie urged. "I'm hungry."

With Mihalis translating Petros' directions, the boys made a long hole in the ground which they filled with sticks. Petros strung the lamb, which the village butcher had cut into chunks, on a long stick. When the fire was going well he and Mihalis held the stick over the trench. Soon the sizzling meat gave off a delicious aroma.

"Boy!" Freddie cried. "That smells yummy!"

"It sure does!" Bert agreed as he passed around hunks of bread.

In a few minutes the meat was cooked and the boys placed the crisp pieces on the bread and began to eat. Nothing had ever tasted so good!

When the meat was eaten, Petros went into the hut and brought out a large bag woven in bright-colored stripes. From it he pulled a small package.

"*Tiri*," he said, holding it toward Bert.

"That's goat cheese," Mihalis explained. "Try some."

Each of the boys broke off a piece. Bert tasted

his. "It's good!" he exclaimed. Freddie agreed.

The boys sat around the dying fire, munching their cheese dessert. As it grew dusky, Petros rose, took up his staff and went down the mountain. He returned shortly, guiding his herd of black goats behind the hut.

Mihalis joined the goatherd. Bert and Freddie could hear them talking together in Greek. Suddenly Bert raised his hand. "Listen!" he said. "I hear a bell. A goat must be lost!"

"Let's find him," Freddie proposed. He jumped up and started to run along the mountain path.

Bert followed. For a while the path was easy to see. The two boys ran on, listening to the tinkle of the goat bell in the distance. The sound led them farther and farther from the hut. By this time it was dark. Bert pulled a flashlight from his pocket. "Maybe that goat doesn't belong to Petros," he said finally. "I think we'd better go back."

At that moment the sound of someone scrambling over the mountain stones just above them came to their ears. Startled, the Bobbsey boys stood still. Bert quickly flashed his light around.

"Who's there?" he called.

CHAPTER IX

THE DISAPPEARING STATUE

AFTER the boys had gone off in the bus with Etsi, Mr. and Mrs. Bobbsey and the three girls ate an early dinner.

When they had finished, Nan asked her mother, "May Flossie and Aliki and I walk outside and look in the shops?"

Mr. and Mrs. Bobbsey had settled down on the terrace to watch the moon rise over the mountain.

"All right," Mrs. Bobbsey replied, "but don't stay too long. It's nearly Flossie's bedtime."

The three girls wandered up the main street of Delphi in the dusk. All the shops were open and brightly lighted. Strains of music came from some of them.

"What darling dolls!" Nan exclaimed, viewing the contents of one window. It was filled with little figures dressed in the costumes of the various Greek provinces.

80

"Let's go in," Aliki suggested. "I'm sure the owner will let us look at them."

The proprietor was very pleasant. He led the girls to a table which was piled with dolls. Nan and Aliki began to pick them up one by one.

While they were doing this, Flossie wandered around the shop, peering at the objects on display. There were hand-woven skirts and blouses, silver pins and bracelets, and trays of post cards.

Suddenly she became aware of a man standing near the rear door. He was rather plump, and his dark eyebrows met over his nose. "Thanos!" Flossie thought and started toward him.

When he saw Flossie, the man turned and hurried out the door. The little girl ran after him.

Meanwhile, the older girls remained intent on the dolls. "I'm going to buy this one!" Nan told Aliki, holding up a small doll with a wide skirt and a tiny shawl over her shoulders. "She'll be perfect for my collection."

As she took out her purse to pay the shop owner she looked around. "Where did Flossie go?" Nan asked Aliki.

"She was back there looking at cards," the Greek girl replied. "But I don't see her now."

"Maybe she's hiding," Nan suggested. The two girls and the proprietor walked around the shop carefully looking into all the corners and under the tables. There was no sign of the little blond girl.

"Flossie must have gone outside," Nan said at last. "Let's look in some of the other shops."

Nan took her doll and they continued their walk up the street, peering into the shops as they went. They had not gone far when Nan suddenly stopped. "There's Flossie!" she cried. "She's trying on shoes!"

Flossie was perched on a stool. A man stood in front of her fitting some strange-looking slippers on her feet. When the two girls walked into the shop Flossie looked up and giggled.

"I thought he was Thanos," she explained, "but he isn't. This shop belongs to him."

"Whatever do you mean, honey?" Nan asked, perplexed.

Flossie explained that she had seen the plump man run from the first shop and had followed him, because he looked like the description of Thanos. But the man had just been hurrying back to his own store which he had left unattended.

"And now he's giving me some of these bee-yoo-ti-ful slippers!" she ended happily. She held up her foot for them to admire the curved toe of the shoe and its large pompon.

"They're Greek shoes," Aliki said. "Many

"He's giving me some of these bee-yoo-ti-ful slippers!"

peasants wear them and so do the evzones."

"What are evzones?" Nan asked curiously.

"They're the soldiers of the Royal Palace Guard. You'll see them in front of the palace in Athens."

Smiling, the shop owner wrapped the little slippers in some gay paper and handed the package to Flossie. When Nan started to pay him the man held up his hands in dismay.

"No, no, no," he protested. "I wish to give them to the little girl!"

Nan and Flossie thanked the man warmly, and the three girls left the shop.

"Wasn't he a nice man?" Flossie asked as she skipped up the street.

"We Greeks love to give presents," Aliki said with a smile. "He wouldn't have liked it if you had paid him for the slippers."

By this time it was dark, and the girls turned back to the hotel.

In the meantime Bert and Freddie stood perfectly still on the mountainside waiting for an answer to Bert's call of "Who's there?" Everything was quiet. Suddenly they heard the high notes of a reed pipe!

"It's Pan!" Freddie cried, looking at Bert in excitement. "It's Pan!"

The older boy was not so sure. "Maybe it's the person we heard before running over the stones up the mountain," Bert said. He flashed his light around, but there was no one in sight.

Freddie had gone up the path a little farther. Now he called to Bert in a choked voice, "Bert! C-come here—quick!"

When Bert reached his little brother, Freddie pointed a shaky finger just ahead. There near the edge of the path lay a white figure. Bert clicked on his flashlight again.

"It's a statue!" he cried.

Freddie looked relieved. He went nearer and peered down at the figure. "It's a statue of Pan!" he cried. "See, he has horns and goat's feet!"

The boy's light revealed that the three-foot marble figure lay at the entrance to a cave in the side of the mountain.

"Let's take Pan back to Petros' hut," Freddie suggested.

Bert agreed, and the boys bent over to pick up the statue. It was too heavy to move!

"We'll need help," Bert remarked. "We'll bring Mihalis and Petros here in the morning."

The brothers made their way back along the path toward the goatherd's hut. After a few minutes the path forked. Bert stopped. "Which way do we go?" he asked.

"I think it's this way," Freddie replied, starting up the left-hand branch.

Bert followed. The boys walked along for some distance, then Bert said uneasily, "It didn't seem this far when we came. I think we made the wrong turn."

But when they went back, Bert's light showed many paths branching off to both sides. "Do you think we're lost, Bert?" Freddie said anxiously.

"Don't worry, Freddie. We can't be too far away from the hut," Bert replied. "Let's shout. Maybe Petros will hear us."

"Hullo!"

"Help!"

They called until they were hoarse. Finally there was an answering shout, and in a few minutes Petros and Mihalis came into view. They were relieved to see the Bobbsey boys.

"I was worried," Mihalis said. "I didn't know where you two had gone."

Bert and Freddie told them about hunting for the goat which they thought was lost. "We didn't find the goat, but we heard Pan's pipes and found his statue!" Freddie said proudly.

Mihalis turned to Petros and told him in Greek what Freddie had said. The goatherd suddenly looked frightened and spoke rapidly to Mihalis.

"Petros says he has heard the pipes," Mihalis translated, "but he cannot understand where the statue came from, and how it got to the cave."

"We'll show it to you in the morning," Bert promised.

The three boys had been following Petros along the paths and finally they arrived at the hut. In a few more minutes they were all wrapped in their blankets and fast asleep.

Freddie woke early the next morning. As he sat up and rubbed his eyes he saw Petros milking a goat just beyond the open side of the hut.

"That looks good," Freddie thought. "I'm thirsty!"

By this time Bert and Mihalis were up. When the goatherd saw that his guests were awake, he called to Mihalis and pointed to a large jar of water and a basin in one corner of the hut.

Mihalis poured water into the bowl, and the boys washed their faces. Stepping out into the sunlight, they saw mugs of goat's milk and big pieces of dark bread laid out on a flat rock.

"This is our breakfast," Mihalis told the Bobbseys.

Bert and Freddie found the milk and bread delicious. Petros watched them eat with a pleased smile. Then he said something in Greek to Mihalis.

"Petros wants to see the statue of Pan now," Mihalis translated.

"Okay. Follow us." Bert and Freddie started

off down the main path with the Greek boys close behind.

Several times Freddie stopped in front of a cave, sure it was the one where they had seen the Pan figure, but each time Bert urged him on. "It was farther than this," Bert persisted.

Finally he said, "I think the cave we want is just around this bend, I remember seeing the curve in the path by the light of my flash last night."

The four boys hurried on. As Freddie turned the corner he cried out.

"Bert! Pan's gone!"

There was no sign of the marble statue. Bert peered into the low cave and examined the ground around it. The statue was not there.

Then Petros pointed to the dirt at the cave entrance. "Donkey tracks!" Mihalis exclaimed. "They're all around here."

"Maybe there are more statues in the cave," Freddie suggested. "I'm going in and look."

The opening was low, and Freddie had to stoop to enter. He crept in and the others could hear him moving around inside. In a few minutes he was back, something hanging from his hand.

It was a dark red sash!

CHAPTER X

A NEW CLUE

BERT took the red sash and examined it closely.
"Where have we seen a sash like this before?" he
said slowly.

Then he answered his own question. "I know!
Freddie, do you remember Dimitris, the man
who came to let us into that factory in Crete?"

Freddie nodded.

"He wore a sash just like this!"

"It's part of the costume of Crete," Mihalis
agreed. "Whoever was in this cave must have
come from there."

Bert looked thoughtful. "If it was Dimitris,
do you suppose Thanos was with him?"

"They could have been the ones in that
wrecked truck!" Mihalis put in excitedly. "You
said you thought it was the one Thanos stole
from Yannis Karilis!"

"But why would Dimitris and Thanos have
been in Delphi?" Bert asked, puzzled.

"Where is our statue of Pan?" Freddie spoke up impatiently.

"The person who left it here in the first place must have returned for it," Mihalis guessed.

"And he must have been the one Freddie and I heard on the mountain last night," Bert said. He placed the red sash in his pants pocket. "This may be a good clue."

The boys started slowly back toward the hut. Then Bert had an idea. "Ask Petros if he knows where Pan's cave is," he said to Mihalis. "The one Alexandros said some people thought was still up here on the mountain."

Petros appeared uneasy when Mihalis put the question to him. But he replied and pointed up the mountain to his right.

"He says the cave's not far from here. Would you like to see it?"

When both Bert and Freddie nodded enthusiastically, Petros left the path and began to make his way up the steep slope. The others followed.

After a ten-minute climb Petros halted before an opening in the rocky mountainside. It was larger than the one where Freddie had found the red sash. The four boys walked in.

"Say!" Bert said admiringly, "this is a neat cave!" He flashed his light around it.

The rock chamber was large, with uneven

walls and ceiling. The floor was dirt. From somewhere in the depths of the cave they could hear the sound of water.

"Maybe the statue of Pan came from here!" Bert suggested. "Let's see what we can find."

Mihalis explained to Petros, and the boys began to explore the cave. Petros proudly produced a flashlight from his woven bag. He and Mihalis walked slowly along one wall while Bert and Freddie took the other side.

"Look at that place, Bert!" Freddie said a few minutes later.

Bert shone his light where Freddie pointed. The ground looked as if it had been dug up recently and loose dirt put back.

"Something has been taken out of here!" Bert cried. "See, the ground's lower than in other spots!"

"Maybe it was the Pan statue!" Freddie exclaimed. "I'll bet it would fit in this space."

Hearing the Bobbseys' excitement, Mihalis and Petros ran up. When Petros saw the dug-up place he looked more uneasy than ever and motioned Mihalis toward the entrance.

"Petros thinks we should leave," Mihalis called to the twins. "Let's go back to the hut and collect our blankets. Then he'll show us the way down to the village."

"Okay," Bert agreed reluctantly. He swept

his flash around the cave once more before following the others out into the sunlight.

Bert, Freddie, and Mihalis thanked Petros for his hospitality, then set out for Delphi. The trip back went much more quickly than the one up. When they reached the hotel, the boys found Mr. and Mrs. Bobbsey and the girls still at breakfast on the terrace.

They listened eagerly to the tale of the boys' adventures on the mountain. "You'd better tell all that to the police, son," Mr. Bobbsey advised Bert.

So, while the others got ready for the morning's sightseeing, Mr. Bobbsey, Bert, and Mihalis walked to headquarters.

The police officer was amazed when he heard the boys' story. "It does sound as if someone had found the ancient statue in Pan's cave and stole it," he said. "I'll send some men to investigate the mountain."

Later, led by Alexandros, Mr. and Mrs. Bobbsey and the children climbed up to the ruins of the old stadium high on the side of Parnassus. The stone seats along one side were still in good condition. The group sat there and listened while Alexandros pointed out the gate at one end where the athletes in olden times had entered. They tried to imagine what the stadium had looked like almost three thousand years ago.

"I wonder if they used to sell hot dogs, peanuts, and popcorn!" Flossie said with a giggle.

Leaving the stadium, the visitors walked down the slope and through the ancient amphitheater. As they went, Alexandros described the life of the people during the time when pilgrimages were made to consult the oracle at Delphi.

Freddie and Flossie were growing tired by the time they entered the museum. They sat down on a marble bench and swung their feet while the others followed the guide through the rooms.

In a little while Nan ran back to the small twins. "We're going to look at the charioteer," she announced.

Flossie's eyes danced. "Now you can see what you were really supposed to look like, Freddie."

The twins caught up with Alexandros in the last room of the museum. There was only one statue here, the tall, bronze figure of the young charioteer. He was dressed in a long flowing robe. One arm was missing, but in his right hand there were still the remains of metal reins.

"This is the most precious object in Delphi," Alexandros told them. "It was found in excellent condition near the Temple of Apollo."

"Look at his eyes!" Flossie exclaimed. "He has stiff eyelashes!"

Alexandros smiled. "They're made of metal."

When they had finished admiring the chariot-eer, the group left the building. Outside, Etsi and the bus were waiting to take them back to the town. "Hey!" Freddie exclaimed. "There's Petros with Etsi!"

Everyone was concerned to see tears running down the goatherd's cheeks.

Bert ran up to the boy. "What's the matter?" he asked, forgetting that Petros did not speak English.

A flood of Greek followed which Alexandros translated. "It seems that when Petros got back to his goats this morning after showing you the way to Delphi, he found his hut pushed over and his goats scattered!"

"Who could have done such a mean thing?" Nan cried.

Alexandros translated a note which Petros handed him. "It says: 'This is what happens when you have snoopy visitors!' He found the paper on the flat rock."

"It must have been the person we heard last night," Bert said indignantly, "the one who stole the statue of Pan from the cave!"

"We'll help you build another hut," Freddie assured the goatherd.

Petros seemed to understand and gave a slight smile.

The little dwelling rested forlornly on its side. Etsi spread the sandwiches on the flat rock, and they all ate quickly.

Then Etsi, Alexandros, and the boys brought armloads of sticks and brush. Everyone worked hard, and soon the crude hut was standing once more. Petros already had rounded up his herd of goats.

"Efcharisto!" he said gratefully when the last stick was in place.

The twins searched for clues to the guilty person, but found none. Petros assured them he would be on guard from now on against any more damage.

Back at the hotel later, the children found their policeman friend waiting for them. He reported that the police had been unable to find out anything about the wrecked truck or the statue of Pan.

Then the officer, whose name was Kladas, went on. "We did find out one thing," he said. "There were two strangers here in the village two days ago. They were not the usual tourists."

"Who were they?" Nan asked eagerly.

"They didn't give their names," Kladas replied. "They bought two donkeys from a farmer at the edge of town. They told him they were artists and were traveling through the country sketching."

"That doesn't sound like much of a clue," Bert said in a discouraged tone.

"Ah," the officer said quickly, "but there is more. One of them wore the red sash of Crete!"

"He did!" Freddie exclaimed. "Then maybe he was in the cave where the Pan statue was. I found a red sash there!"

"They could be the men who dug up the figure in Pan's cave and left it at the entrance to the other one," Nan surmised.

"And also pushed over the hut and left the note for Petros!" Bert added.

"Perhaps," Kladas said with a smile. "At any rate, we will continue to search on the mountain. I am sorry you are going away, because you have told us many things."

The Bobbseys, too, were sorry to leave the beautiful spot, but Etsi said they were to board a ferry to cross the Gulf of Corinth the next morning at nine o'clock.

The ride down to Itea, the little town where the boat docked, was over a winding, narrow road.

"We're going down to those olive trees!" Flossie exclaimed as she peered from the window.

"These trunks are huge!" Mrs. Bobbsey remarked in surprise as they drove through the ancient grove.

"Some of these trees are over a thousand years old," Etsi told her.

"Everything in Greece is old!" Freddie observed.

"Even the ferryboat!" Bert said with a grin as Etsi drove onto the dock and stopped.

The boat waiting for them was an old troop-landing ship. It carried cars, trucks, and buses on its main deck. The only seats seemed to be in a small cabin forward and on a narrow deck surrounding the bridge.

As Etsi maneuvered the little bus into a space on the deck a sailor came up to take his ticket. Etsi pulled a piece of blue paper from his pocket.

Bert, who was seated beside him, stared at it. "That's like the paper I found in the wrecked truck!" he exclaimed.

CHAPTER XI

THE DANCING DOLPHINS

"WHAT paper?" asked Mihalis, who was seated behind Bert.

Quickly Bert reached into his pocket and pulled out a crumpled piece of blue paper. "This one," he said. "I picked it up from the floor of that truck and stuck it in my pocket. I forgot all about it till now!"

Etsi took the slip and examined it. "It's a ticket for this ferry, all right," he remarked.

"Then whoever was in the truck planned to cross the Gulf here!" Bert said excitedly.

"That was the day before yesterday," Mihalis pointed out.

"Let's ask if the ticket taker noticed anyone unusual on the ferry," Bert suggested.

The two boys jumped from the bus and ran back to the young sailor who was collecting the tickets. The others got out and walked up a narrow stair to the upper deck.

The sailor looked surprised at the boys' question.

"Strange passengers?" he repeated. "I can't think of any." Then he reconsidered.

"Perhaps you mean the two men in that old car," he said.

"What did they look like?" Bert asked eagerly.

The sailor shrugged. "Nothing unusual," he replied. "I think one wore a mustache."

"What made you notice them?" Mihalis persisted.

The sailor replied that the car the two men had was very old—an open model. "Then, instead of going up on deck or into the lounge," he added, "those men sat down here in their car during the crossing. And it takes almost three hours!"

"Was there anything else odd?" Bert asked.

Again the sailor thought. "Well, they did have a big bundle in the back seat. It was covered by a rug. I couldn't see what it was."

"The statue!" Bert cried triumphantly.

"But we don't know where they might be now!" Mihalis reminded him.

Bert turned to the curious sailor. "Did you notice which way they went when the ferry docked?"

"They turned east toward Corinth," was the reply.

"That's also in the direction of Athens," Mihalis remarked. He explained to Bert that the Gulf of Corinth separated the main part of Greece from the southern part which was called the Peloponnesos. "Corinth is in the Peloponnesos at the eastern end of the Gulf, and from there to Athens it's only about ninety-four kilometers," he went on.

Bert figured quickly. "That's almost sixty miles, isn't it?"

"Yes," replied Mihalis. "We'll be going that way."

The Greek boy said that his father had arranged for them to visit the Isthmian ruins and meet the archaeologist there, who was a friend of his. "The ruins are quite near Corinth," he explained.

"The two men might have stopped along the way," Bert said hopefully. "Let's watch for them."

The boys joined the others on the deck. They had found seats and were watching the small islands the ferry passed on its way out into the Gulf. Bert and Mihalis related their talk with the sailor to Nan and the small twins, who listened with interest.

Presently Freddie and Flossie grew restless. They wandered over to the rail and looked down at a small open deck space at the bow. Several Greek families were there, including some children who were playing a game.

"Let's go down," Freddie suggested.

"Okay," Flossie agreed and started for the stairs.

"I'll come too," Aliki said and followed the small twins to the lower deck. There they were welcomed by the friendly children.

Aliki talked to them quickly in Greek, then turned to Freddie and Flossie. "They're playing a game where the one who is 'It' puts a ring in the hand of one of the children in the circle. The others try to guess who has the ring."

Flossie looked at Freddie. "That's like our game, 'Button, Button, Who's Got the Button?' "

Aliki told the Greek children that the American twins knew the game. The youngsters smiled and quickly decided on Aliki to be It. She took her place in the center of the circle, the ring clasped between her palms. Freddie and Flossie sat on the deck with the other children.

Amid a good many giggles Aliki went from one to another placing her hands between their palms. When she had finished, she chose Flossie to be first to guess who had the ring.

Flossie pointed to a dark-eyed Greek boy with black curly hair. With a grin he spread open his hands to show he did not have the ring. Then he guessed the little girl sitting next to him. She opened her empty hands, and the game went on until it was discovered that Freddie had the ring!

At that moment a man on the top deck cried out and pointed to the water. The children below all ran to the rail. There, very near the boat, were three dolphins. In unison, they leaped from the water, then dived back in. Behind them were three more of the playful creatures.

"They're dancing!" Flossie cried in delight. "They look like those fish on the wall of the queen's room in that old palace we saw!"

The children watched the frisking fish until the ferry left them far behind, then turned back to the ring game.

It seemed no time at all before Mrs. Bobbsey called Freddie and Flossie. The ferry was coming into the dock at a little town on the south shore of the Gulf. A short while later, they were all in the bus driving along the coastal road toward Corinth.

"I'm hungry, Mommy!" Flossie exclaimed when they had gone only a short way.

"Me too!" the others chorused.

"Is there any place where we can get lunch, Etsi?" Mr. Bobbsey asked.

The driver nodded. "There's a very good roadside *taverna* just ahead," he replied.

A few miles farther on, Etsi turned off the road and stopped under a large tree.

"Our restaurant," he announced.

The Bobbseys saw a low, white stucco building. In front was a wide, paved terrace shaded by a grape arbor. Tables were set out on the terrace.

"Look!" cried Nan, pointing to one side.

There on a stand was a metal trough filled with charcoal. Over this two men were turning a whole lamb on a spit. The roasting meat smelled delicious.

At this moment the proprietor, wearing a long white apron, came up to welcome the visitors. With a flourish of his hand he indicated a large table at the edge of the terrace.

"Your meal will be ready in a few minutes," he said in English. "Please sit down."

"What's that?" Flossie asked curiously, looking at a mound of light-colored earth shaped like a beehive, which stood nearby.

"That is our oven," the man replied. "My wife is baking bread. It is almost done."

While everyone else took seats, Bert and Freddie wandered over to the spot where the meat was being cooked. One of the men looked up with a smile. He held out the end of the spit to Bert. "You help?" he said in halting English.

"Let me too!" Freddie pleaded.

The other man handed over his end of the spit

to the little boy, and Bert and Freddie carefully turned the sizzling meat.

In a few minutes the proprietor's wife bustled from the doorway. She carried a long-handled wooden shovel. When she saw the two boys at the spit she looked amused. The woman walked up to the table where the rest of the party sat.

"Would the young American ladies like to help also?" she asked.

Nan and Flossie nodded eagerly. They followed the woman over to the beehive oven. She opened the metal door and thrust the shovel into the dark interior. The next second she lifted out a long loaf of delicately browned bread and carefully dropped it onto a flat stone.

Then she handed the shovel to Nan, who managed to get a loaf onto the shovel. She pulled it out, and the bread landed upside down.

"Good, Nan!" Flossie praised her sister. "Now it's my turn!"

Flossie grasped the wooden handle firmly and pushed the shovel into the oven. The next moment she drew it out proudly. The loaf was safely in the middle of the scoop.

"Ouch!" Freddie screamed suddenly. A drop of hot fat from the meat had struck his hand.

At the sound Flossie jumped. The bread flew from the shovel and landed on the stone floor!

Tears came to the little girl's eyes. "I—I'm sorry," she said.

The bread flew from the shovel

The woman patted Flossie's shoulder. "Don't worry," she said. "We always lose one loaf."

By this time all the food was ready. The twins rejoined the party around the table. The owner of the restaurant now served plates of roast lamb, sliced red tomatoes, cucumbers, bowls of olives and potatoes fried in olive oil. For dessert there were big slices of ripe melon.

"Mm-mm!" Flossie said. "I love Greek lunches."

Her family agreed everything was delicious. "And this melon is wonderful," Mrs. Bobbsey added.

At that moment a man standing beside the door began to play an accordion. Immediately the restaurant owner and the two men who had been turning the spit joined arms and swung into a dance. The other Greek people on the terrace clapped their hands in time to the music.

"Join us!" the proprietor called with a laugh. Mihalis jumped up, pulling Bert and Freddie with him. In another minute they had caught the rhythm of the dance and were swaying and jumping with the others. Mr. and Mrs. Bobbsey and the girls applauded heartily.

Finally Etsi stood up and regretfully announced that if they were to reach Athens by evening they must go on. After many thanks and good-bys to the proprietor and his wife, the group piled into the bus and drove off.

"That was fun," Freddie remarked. "I wish we could do things like that at home!"

"We Greeks are very gay people," Etsi told him. "We love to have a good time!"

A few miles farther on, Bert sat forward and peered intently out the window. "Look! That old open car ahead!" he said excitedly. "There are two men in it and a big bundle on the back seat!"

"Do you think they're the same men who were on the ferry?" Mihalis asked.

"Pass them, Etsi!" Nan urged. "Let's see what they look like!"

Obligingly Etsi speeded up. But the old car did the same. The road was not very wide. Every time Etsi felt it safe to pass, the car ahead would go faster.

Suddenly the old car began to bump up and down. As it pulled to the side of the road, the bus passengers saw that one of the tires was flat.

Etsi halted. Quickly, he, Bert, and Mihalis jumped out.

"The driver has a mustache!" Bert noted excitedly.

Etsi and Mihalis walked up to the man, who by now was outside looking at the tire. While they talked to him in Greek, Bert moved close to the bundle in the back seat.

Then looking cautiously around, he reached in and slowly raised the cover.

CHAPTER XII

RED AND GREEN MEN

"OH!" Bert exclaimed in dismay as he peered under the old rug. Instead of the Pan statue which he had expected to see, there was a large metal container with Greek letters on it!

Mihalis looked over Bert's shoulder. "It's only olive oil!" he said with a grin. "These men say they didn't come across on the ferry. They're from farther south, near Olympia."

"We were following a false clue that time," Bert admitted ruefully as he turned to help with the tire.

The men became very friendly while changing the wheel and said that they had just been testing their old car when they had speeded up to prevent Etsi from passing them. Everyone laughed, then the men thanked Etsi and the boys for their help and drove away.

Not long afterward the little bus went through the small town of modern Corinth and out into the country beyond. It bumped over some dirt roads and finally drew up before a low house surrounded by tall cypress trees.

"This is the home of my father's archaeologist friend," said Mihalis.

A middle-aged man in a Panama hat came out to greet them. "I am Mr. Freeman," he said. "Mr. Gorzako wrote me that you would like to see some of our excavations."

Mr. Bobbsey introduced himself and his family. Then they all followed the archaeologist across a field and down some crude steps into the excavations. As they walked, Mr. Freeman pointed out foundations of ancient buildings, including a theater, which he had unearthed.

Finally he paused in a large flat area. "You are now standing on the place where the Isthmian games were held over two thousand years ago," he announced. "They took place every two years in honor of Poseidon, the Greek god of the sea."

"Our teacher told us about the Greek games," Bert remarked. "We tried to have some at our school, but they turned out sort of funny."

Nan had been looking at the ground. Now she asked, "What was this hole used for?" She pointed to a waist-deep, round pit hollowed out of the rock.

Mr. Freeman smiled. "We think we've figured

that out," he said. "Do you see these marks in the stone?" He pointed to some lines which ran from the edge of the pit across the rock.

When the children nodded, the archaeologist picked up three poles of polished wood which lay on the ground nearby. These were fastened together by a series of pulleys and cord. As he set the poles in small square holes in the stone, he went on, "We think the starter for the foot races stood in that pit. The runners lined up against a barrier such as this cross-pole. When the starter pulled one of the strings from his place in the pit, the cross-piece dropped and the racers were off! The lines in the stone were made by the constant friction of the cord."

Seeing the interested looks on the children's faces, he asked, "Would you like to try it?"

They nodded eagerly. Mr. Freeman threaded the cord through the pulley and gave the end to Bert, who had climbed down into the pit. Freddie, Flossie, and Aliki took their places at the cross-pole.

"One—two—three," Nan counted. At the word *"Go,"* Bert pulled the string, the pole dropped, and the three children raced over the stone surface. Aliki reached the end of the course first and was declared the winner.

"She should win because she's Greek," Freddie said generously.

Shortly after that the Bobbseys thanked Mr. Freeman and said good-by. The bus continued its journey toward Athens. Etsi stopped on the bridge which spanned the Corinth Canal.

"This canal joins the Gulf of Corinth and the Saronic Gulf," he explained. "Before it was built at the end of the last century all ships had to go around the Peloponnesos to get from the Aegean to the Ionian Sea."

The Americans peered down at the narrow strip of water running between the steep, straight walls. "It looks just about wide enough for my toy sailboat," Freddie observed.

Dinner was waiting when the party finally reached the Gorzako home later that evening. Mihalis and Aliki amazed their parents with the story of the wrecked truck, the disappearing statue of Pan, and the other mysterious happenings.

"You certainly had an exciting time!" the Greek ship builder commented with a smile. "I'm particularly interested in the statue. It sounds as if that gang of thieves may be operating around Delphi too. I've heard that the government suspects antiquities are also being stolen from the island of Delos."

"Really?" said Nan, then added, "Is Delos very far away?"

"About an eight-hour run by boat," Mr.

Gorzako replied. "If you'd like to see it I'm sure you could stay with my friends, Mr. and Mrs. Pappas. They have a house on Mykonos near Delos."

"That would be great!" said Bert.

"All right," their host declared. "I'll write to Mr. Pappas tonight, and I can send you all over there in one of my boats. I know Aliki and Mihalis will want to go with you." He smiled at his children, who nodded delightedly.

"Yes, Mykonos is keen!" Mihalis declared.

The next morning it was arranged that Etsi would drive the twins and Mihalis into Athens. Aliki was going to visit a friend. The men had a business appointment, and their wives were invited out to luncheon.

"Etsi has some errands to do for me in town," Mrs. Gorzako said. "He can drop you children off there, and pick you up later."

When they reached Athens Etsi let the children out near the public gardens. He drove away, promising to meet them later on.

As they started across the street Flossie pointed to the traffic light and giggled. "Look! It's a little green man!"

"No, he's a red man!" Freddie cried.

The others studied the lights as they changed. The green showed a little man walking, and when the light was red the little man stood still.

"We Athenians call the green man Grigoris and the red man Stamatis," Mihalis explained. "We make a pun that way because in Greek *stamato* means 'I stop' and *grigora* means 'quick.'"

Nan laughed. "I like that," she said. "Now Grigoris is walking so we can be quick!"

When they had reached the other side of the street Mihalis continued his story. "On St. Grigoris Day some young Athenians decorate the lights with flowers to show that they like Grigoris, who lets them cross the street, better than Stamatis, who makes them stop!"

"We should decorate the traffic lights in Lakeport!" Bert declared, grinning.

By this time they had turned into the gardens.

"The Royal Palace is just across the street where you'll see the Evzone guards," Mihalis pointed out. "Father gave me a letter to deliver to a friend of his who lives nearby. You might like to wait in the gardens until I get back. I won't be long."

When Mihalis had left, Bert and Nan walked into the gardens. Freddie and Flossie stood on the sidewalk looking across the street at the palace grounds surrounded by a high iron fence. The palace itself was out of sight.

"Look at the lady standing in front of that little house," Flossie said in surprise.

"That's not a lady, it's a man!" Freddie replied scornfully. "Mihalis said he's a guard."

"Well, he's wearing skirts!" his sister protested.

The small twins crossed the street to see the guard. The man, who stood at attention in front of a small white sentry box, wore a very full short white skirt, a white shirt with long pleated sleeves, and an embroidered, sleeveless black velvet jacket. On his head was a round red cap with a long black tassel. He wore white stockings and black slippers with turned-up toes and black pompons.

"His slippers are like the ones that nice man gave me!" Flossie exclaimed in delight. "I want to take his picture."

But when she showed the guard her little camera and asked if she might snap him, he stared straight ahead and made no reply.

"I think it's all right, Flossie," Freddie assured her. "He's not s'posed to smile or say anything."

Flossie snapped the picture. Then Freddie had an idea. "You stand next to him and look important. I'll take a picture of you both."

Flossie stood very straight beside the motionless guard, and Freddie clicked the shutter.

In the meantime Bert and Nan had strolled farther into the gardens. They sat down on a

Flossie stood very straight beside the motionless guard

bench while Bert changed the film in his camera. A minute later they looked up to see a small boy standing in front of them. He had a tray suspended from a strap around his neck. On the tray were many little packages of nuts. He held out a package toward Bert.

"They look good," Nan said. "Let's buy some." She reached into her purse for some coins.

Suddenly the boy began to chatter in Greek. He seemed to be trying to tell them something.

Bert looked at the lad closely, and turned in surprise to his twin. "I think he's the boy we saw at Yannis Karilis' fur factory!"

When the boy heard the word Karilis he began to speak even more urgently. Bert and Nan listened with keen attention. Finally a familiar word caught Nan's ear. "I think he said something about Thanos!" she exclaimed.

The boy nodded vehemently. "Thanos! Thanos!" he repeated and made gestures toward the street.

"Maybe he knows where Thanos is and wants us to go with him," Bert suggested.

As if understanding, the boy took Bert by the sleeve and started toward the entrance.

"You go with him," Nan urged. "I'll wait here for Mihalis and Freddie and Flossie."

CHAPTER XIII

WORRY BEADS

"OKAY," Bert agreed. "I'll follow him and see what he's so excited about." He ran after the little nut vendor, who had walked ahead and was waiting at the garden entrance.

The boy appeared delighted that Bert was coming. The two hurried on down the street.

"Where are you going?" came a call in English from the other side of the street.

Bert looked over to see Mihalis standing at the curb, a puzzled expression on his face. "I think this boy knows where Thanos is," Bert called back.

"Wait! I'll talk to him." Mihalis ran across and began to speak to the younger lad in Greek. There followed a long conversation, with the strange boy using many gestures.

Finally Mihalis turned to Bert. "This boy's name is Spiros," he began. "He works for Yannis Karilis and saw you at the fur factory."

"That's right," Bert agreed. "Nan and I remember him."

"And you were right. He does think he knows where Thanos is." Mihalis went on to explain that Spiros had caught a glimpse of Thanos early that morning. He had run to the factory to tell Yannis but learned that the fur man had left for northern Greece on a business trip.

"Spiros has been selling nuts since the factory closed down. When he recognized you and Nan in the park he remembered hearing Mr. Karilis tell you about Thanos. He wants to show you where he thinks Thanos lives."

"Good!" Bert said, smiling at Spiros, who was waiting impatiently.

"Don't you think you should go to the police?" Mihalis said in a worried tone. "Thanos may be dangerous."

"I'll just find out if he's really where Spiros thinks he is, then we can get the police," Bert promised.

"I'll stay in the garden with Nan," Mihalis said. "We'll meet you there."

Spiros now led Bert at a fast pace through some winding, narrow streets. "Plaka," the boy said with a smile, looking around him.

"I guess that's the name of this district," Bert said to himself.

Many of the streets were too narrow for automobiles and very few had sidewalks. Tall houses rose straight up from the street. Some had crumbling stairways up their sides.

Finally Spiros stopped before a shabby-looking stucco house and knocked on the door. An elderly woman with a black cloth over her head answered. She shook her head in reply to a question from the boy.

Spiros seemed to persist in his queries and the two held a lively discussion in Greek. The boy turned to Bert and tried to explain with gestures what the woman had said.

"Thanos," he said, pointing to himself.

Bert nodded.

"Thanos," the boy repeated, then added, *"Kali andamosi,"* and walked off a few steps, waving as he did.

"That means good-by," Bert told himself. "He means Thanos has gone away." He looked questioningly at Spiros and repeated, "Where?"

The boy seemed to understand. He moved his arms and hands in a waving motion, then leaned forward and back from his waist with his fists doubled.

Bert thought a minute. Then his face cleared. "A boat!" he cried. "You mean Thanos has gone off on a boat!"

Now Spiros looked uncertain. Quickly Bert pulled a notebook from his pocket and drew a sketch of a rowboat. He handed it to Spiros.

"Nae, nae!" The Greek boy nodded his head

Quickly Bert drew a sketch of a rowboat

vigorously. He stretched out his arms full length
to indicate that the boat was larger than a rowboat and made a gesture of fishing. When Bert
smiled in recognition, Spiros took the sketch and
pencil. Carefully, where the name of the boat
would be, he drew the Greek letters ΒΥΛΛ
and handed back the notebook.

By this time the woman had gone inside and
slammed the door. Spiros motioned to Bert and
they began to walk back to the park.

When they arrived they found Freddie and
Flossie watching some swans on a small lake
while Nan and Mihalis paced nervously up and
down the path.

"Bert!" Nan cried, running toward her twin.
"I was afraid something had happened to you!
Are you all right!"

"Sure!" Bert grinned. "I didn't find Thanos,
but we have a clue. Ask Spiros what that woman
at the house said, will you, Mihalis?"

After questioning Spiros at length, Mihalis
said the woman had told the boy that Thanos
rented a room in her house. Sometimes he went
out in a fishing boat with a friend. Thanos had
told her that morning he was going on the boat
and would be away several days. The name of
the boat was *The Bull*.

"That's the name Spiros printed on your
sketch, Bert," Mihalis explained.

"Why does he keep saying *nae, nae* all the

time?" Nan asked, puzzled. "Doesn't he think you're telling the story right?"

"Nae is Greek for yes," Mihalis replied. "Did you think he was saying no?"

Nan laughed and admitted she had.

"I think we should go to the police now," Bert declared.

The twins and Mihalis each bought a bag of nuts from Spiros, and Bert thanked him for his help. Then Mihalis hailed a taxi to take them to headquarters. There they talked to an officer who knew about the theft of Yannis Karilis' fur.

Bert told him that Thanos could probably be found on a fishing vessel called *The Bull.*

"We'll look for the boat at once," the officer assured him. "Thank you for the information."

Outside the building Mihalis suggested that it was time for lunch. The twins eagerly agreed. "How would you like to eat at a sidewalk restaurant?" the Greek boy asked.

"Yes! Let's!" Flossie cried.

"We'll go to Constitution Square," Mihalis proposed. "That's the center of Athens."

A short time later the five children sat at a table facing the park in the middle of the square. "Will you have some octopus?" Mihalis asked.

"Octopus!" Nan cried. "Do you *eat* it?"

Mihalis looked surprised. "Of course," he

replied. "It's very good. I think I'll order some."

Thinking of the odd, many-armed creature she had seen in aquariums, Nan shuddered. "I think I'd rather have something else," she decided.

The Bobbseys all ordered broiled fish, which proved to be brown and tasty-looking. Mihalis persuaded Flossie to try a piece of his stewed octopus.

"Mmm," she said a moment later, "it *is* good!"

After that Mihalis had to order another plateful because each of the twins wanted some. They had just finished eating as Etsi drove up to the curb to take them back to the beach.

When they arrived, the twins and Mihalis gave an excited account of their day in Athens. The grownups and Aliki were astonished to hear the news of Thanos.

"I hope the police find him," said Aliki.

"I wish *we* could," Freddie declared.

Mrs. Bobbsey smiled. "After all that excitement, it would be a good idea for you twins to rest before dinner," she said. "Mr. Gorzako is taking us to the Acropolis tonight."

"Tonight?" Bert asked in surprise.

Mr. Gorzako explained that the Acropolis was open on the three nights when the moon was fullest. "Our visitors consider this the most romantic time to view the Acropolis," he said.

"It sounds dreamy!" Nan sighed.

Shortly before ten o'clock that evening the Gorzako and Bobbsey families set out for the city. The moon was high in the sky as Etsi drove up the slope toward the Acropolis and parked on the terrace just below the entrance.

"We should all keep together," Mr. Gorzako advised as they walked up toward the ruins in the moonlight. "But if we get separated we will meet back here at the car in about an hour."

The children followed the adults up the path to the Propylaea, through the old entranceway and out onto the rocky plateau. It was an eerie sight. The moonlight caused the marble columns to cast long shadows over the area.

Occasionally a cloud would obscure the moon and the plateau would be completely dark. "It's sort of scary," Flossie whispered. She moved closer to her mother and took her hand.

"It's so quiet," Nan said wonderingly as she looked over the crowd of tourists. The beauty of the scene seemed to have silenced their usual chatter.

Presently Nan wandered off by herself to look down on the lights of the city. A few minutes later she walked back toward the Parthenon. As she stepped between a pair of the huge columns, she spotted two men standing in the pillars' shadow. Nan could just make out the dark shape of a fur hat which one man held in his hand.

"The fur plates will be shipped tomorrow," Nan heard one man say in English.

"Fur plates!" Nan thought, instantly alert.

The other man replied, but in such a low voice Nan could not make out the words. But she did hear the *click-click* of his worry beads. "The men must be Greek," she said to herself. "That thin one—could he be Dimitris?"

Cautiously Nan moved nearer, but as she did the men walked off, still talking earnestly. At that moment Bert grabbed his twin's arm. Nan jumped violently.

"What's the matter, Sis?" he asked teasingly. "Think I was a ghost?"

Quickly Nan told him about the men and what she had overhead. "Where are they?" Bert asked.

"It's hard to tell in the dark," Nan replied. "I think they went toward the museum."

"I'll walk over that way and see if I can find them," Bert volunteered. He moved off across the moonlit plateau.

Nan started to follow. At that moment a cloud floated across the moon. She paused to get her bearings. Then suddenly in front of her loomed the figure of a man. He stopped. She could hear the *click-click* of worry beads!

Nan ran forward and grasped the man's arm!

CHAPTER XIV

A BEACH DISCOVERY

"WHAT—" the man began in surprise as he wheeled around to look at Nan.

It was Mr. Gorzako!

"Oh! I—I'm so sorry," Nan stammered, embarrassed. "I thought you were someone else!" She explained about the conversation she had overheard between the two men. "One of them had worry beads, so when I heard yours—" She paused.

Mr. Gorzako laughed. "That's not a very good clue, I'm afraid," he reminded her. "Many Greek men carry worry beads. But come, perhaps we can find these men." He took Nan's arm and guided her over the rocky ground.

Nan and her host paused beside two men who were talking earnestly in Greek while one busily clicked his beads. "They're debating about the Parthenon," Mr. Gorzako said with a chuckle.

The two walked on searching for the men Nan

had seen. They had no success. Finally they met Bert. He, too, had been unable to find anyone who looked suspicious.

"It probably wasn't Dimitris anyway," Nan said sadly.

On the drive back to the beach house the weather changed suddenly. The moon disappeared behind a huge cloud bank and the whole sky turned a threatening black.

Toward morning Bert woke to hear wind and rain lashing against the house. He sat up in bed, then jumped out and ran across the room to close the windows. Peering out, he saw that the sea was a churning mass of whitecaps. The waves, dashing against some rocks at the edge of the beach, sent spray high up onto the terrace.

"Boy!" Bert thought. "Some storm! I don't see how the fishing boat Thanos is on could weather this!"

The storm continued all that day, and no one left the house. Mrs. Gorzako brought out games and puzzles for everyone to play.

They had such a good time that before she dropped off to sleep that night Flossie said, "I like this storm. It's fun."

But the next morning the sun was out in a cloudless blue sky. After breakfast the children ran to the beach to see how much damage the storm had caused.

The lawn and beach areas were strewn with broken branches and leaves from the palm trees. Several trees had been uprooted and the highway behind the house was littered with debris.

Everyone pitched in to clear the beach of some of the trash which covered it. Nan, as she worked, strolled along the sand and peered at the unusual shells tossed up by the storm. She had wandered some distance from the house when she suddenly stopped.

"Goodness, what's that?" she said, startled. Ahead of her, partially covered by sand and seaweed, was a large helmeted head. As she peered at it more closely Nan saw that it was made of bronze turned green by the sea water.

"How did it ever get here?" she wondered. "Yoo-hoo!" she called to the rest of the children far down the beach. "Come see what I've found!"

At this point the beach was very near the road. As Nan waited for the others, a tan car came to a screeching halt. The next minute two men jumped from it and ran to the beach.

Before Nan could recover from her astonishment they had picked up the bronze head, dumped it into a large basket which they carried, and run back to the car with their burden.

"Wait!" Nan cried. "Where are you going with that?"

"Wait!" Nan cried. "Where are you going with that?"

The men did not pause and in another second the car roared off down the road.

"What happened?" Bert demanded as he reached his twin. "Who were those men?"

By this time Mihalis, Aliki, and the small twins had joined them. Nan described the helmeted head which she had seen in the sand.

"That sounds like a real treasure!" Mihalis exclaimed. "And those men got away with it! The bronze head must have been in the sea for many years. Perhaps it was on a ship which sank and yesterday's storm washed it up," he concluded.

"What did those men look like?" Flossie piped up.

Nan confessed that everything had happened so fast she did not have a chance to notice much about the two. "They both had caps pulled down over their faces," she said, "and I think one of them had a mustache."

When the children reported the occurrence to Mr. Gorzako he called headquarters at once and gave them a full report. "There isn't much to go on," he admitted, "but at least the police can keep a watch out for that tan car."

That afternoon Mr. Gorzako had a letter from his friend Mr. Pappas, who lived on the island of Mykonos. Mr. Pappas wrote that he and his wife would be delighted to have Mr. and

Mrs. Bobbsey, their children and Mihalis and
Aliki stay with them and suggested they come to
Mykonos the next day.

"If you'd like," their host said to Mrs. Bobbsey, "I can have my skipper Stefanos run you
over there tomorrow."

The Bobbseys all eagerly agreed. So, shortly
before noon the next day, they boarded the
Gorzakos' launch for the trip to the island. The
twins liked Stefanos immediately. He was tall
with a black bristling mustache and snapping
black eyes.

He showed the Bobbseys over the trim craft,
then they all settled down in lounge chairs on the
small afterdeck. They passed many fishing
boats.

"We call them *caiques*," Stefanos told his
passengers. "They have motors as well as
sails."

"Did you ever see a fishing boat called *The
Bull?*" Bert asked.

"Yes, I have seen it in the harbor at Piraeus,"
the skipper replied. "It is an old boat, but I'm
told it has a fast new motor. Do you know
it?"

Bert told him about Thanos and how he was
supposed to have gone off on *The Bull*.

"It is very possible," Stefanos agreed. "I have
heard stories that *The Bull* has carried some
shady cargo in addition to fish!"

"I wish we could catch it," Freddie said wistfully.

"We'll keep a lookout," Stefanos promised.

But although they all watched for a boat named *The Bull,* they did not see it.

Late in the afternoon Stefanos pointed ahead. "There is Mykonos," he said.

The Bobbseys saw a brown island rising from the deep blue sea. Many small white houses were built on the hill behind the crescent-shaped harbor. They sparkled in the sunlight.

"It's bee-yoo-ti-full!" Flossie cried.

The launch was moored to the dock, and with a flourish Stefanos helped them all ashore. As they stepped onto the pier a man came up to Mr. Bobbsey.

"Kalimera," he said with a big smile which showed his white teeth. Then in broken English he continued, "I am Costa. Mr. Pappas send two taxis for you."

With a sweep of his hand he indicated two cars parked at the end of the dock. They were old models but clean and shining.

The children waved good-by to Stefanos and followed the grownups. Beyond a narrow strip of sand was a wide paved area bordered by shops and restaurants. Many tourists in bright-colored clothes walked in and out of the shops.

"It looks very gay!" Nan exclaimed happily.

"There are cruise ships anchored outside," Costa said. "Visitors come ashore for few hours, then leave."

When they reached the cars it was decided that Freddie and Flossie would ride with Mr. and Mrs. Bobbsey while the older twins went with Mihalis and Aliki.

"Does Mr. Pappas live very far away?" Freddie asked as he climbed into the seat beside the driver.

For answer the man pointed up to a large white house atop a ridge in back of the town. He drove away from the harbor and turned onto a dirt road that ran uphill.

"We don't go through town?" Mrs. Bobbsey asked in disappointment.

"Streets too narrow and crooked for cars," Costa replied. "Only donkeys can get through."

Then, seeing the bewildered expressions of his passengers, he explained. "Many years ago pirates sailed in these waters. They would land and rob the people. So Mykonos make streets narrow and crooked so pirates get lost!"

"Wow!" Freddie exclaimed, his eyes dancing with excitement. "I wish I'd been here when the pirates were around!"

A few minutes later Costa drew up before the white stucco house. Its front door opened directly onto the road. Waiting to greet the group were Mr. and Mrs. Pappas. He had graying hair and a flashing smile. Mrs. Pappas was somewhat plump, with black hair pulled back into a knot.

"Welcome to Mykonos!" Mr. Pappas exclaimed in excellent English. "We hope you will make our house your home while you are here," he said cordially.

Mihalis and Aliki, who were old friends of the Pappas family, introduced the Bobbseys. Mrs. Pappas led the visitors up a narrow stairway to an upper floor and showed them into bright, airy bedrooms.

"When you are ready," she said, "Come out onto the terrace. That is where we live most of the time!"

Later they all met on the terrace. It extended the length of the house and overlooked the town and the harbor. In one corner the table was set for the evening meal and comfortable chairs and sofas were scattered about.

Mounted on the iron railing which surrounded the terrace was a telescope.

"Say, that's neat!" Bert said admiringly when he spotted it. "I bet you could see a lot from here!"

"It is my husband's hobby!" Mrs. Pappas said with a laugh. "He keeps track of all the doings in the harbor through that telescope!"

"It's quiet now," Mr. Pappas remarked.

"Most of the tourists have left the island on the cruise ships. But if you'd like to, we'll look through the 'scope after dinner."

The children all nodded eagerly.

The meal was delicious. When the first course turned out to be octopus, Flossie eyed Mihalis mischievously and ate every bite on her plate. Finally, when they had finished the dessert of fresh strawberries, Mr. Pappas pushed back his chair.

"I think it's still light enough to get a good view of the waterfront," he remarked as he walked over to the telescope. "I'll adjust it and then you can all have a look."

He peered into the telescope and twisted a few knobs. Then suddenly he exclaimed in surprise, "How strange!"

CHAPTER XV

THE BOAT CHASE

"WHAT'S strange, Mr. Pappas?" Nan asked.

"See that boat just headed away from shore?"
Mr. Pappas pointed.

Everyone crowded to the railing of the terrace
and peered seaward. A small motor launch was
making its way out of the harbor.

"Yes," Mihalis answered for all. "Is that
unusual?"

Mr. Pappas explained that when he had
looked through the telescope he had seen a man
step into the boat from the very end of the pier.
"The launch appears to be heading for Delos,"
he declared. "No one goes over there at night!"

"Delos is the island where Mr. Gorzako said
the government suspects antiquities are being
stolen," Bert said excitedly.

"But *why* doesn't anyone go there at night?"
Freddie wanted to know.

Mr. Pappas told them that except for a caretaker and sometimes a few archaeologists, no one lived on Delos. "There are only ruins there now," he said. "In ancient days it was thought to have been the birthplace of Apollo."

"He was the one who played being a dolphin!" Flossie said with a giggle.

Smiling, Mr. Pappas continued. "Delos was a rich and busy city at one time, about two thousand years ago. Unfortunately it was destroyed by invaders and never rebuilt."

"It must be spooky at night!" Nan remarked with a shudder.

"That's why I can't understand the boat heading that way," Mr. Pappas remarked. Then he shrugged, and arranged the telescope so that his guests could scan the waterfront.

The twins could clearly see the tables and chairs in front of the restaurants, full of late diners. Also the few men strolling up and down the pavement. Everything seemed to be quiet.

"I believe Stefanos plans to take you over to Delos tomorrow afternoon," their host said. "Perhaps in the morning you would like to explore our town. It is an easy walk down."

The next morning Mr. and Mrs. Bobbsey decided to do some shopping while the children walked around town. "If we don't run into you before," Mrs. Bobbsey said, "we'll meet you back at the house at lunch time." She waved good-by and went into a small shop filled with hand-woven clothes.

"Let's go see the Church of the Cat," Aliki suggested impishly, with a wink at her brother.

"The Church of the Cat!" Flossie repeated. "What's that?"

Mihalis told the Bobbseys that there were over three hundred churches on the small island and the Church of the Cat was one of them.

"Are there enough people to go to them all?" Nan asked wonderingly.

"Most of the churches are little," Aliki replied. "They are big enough to hold only a few people at a time. You see, the men on this island fish for a living. Often when they are out in a storm they are afraid they will be drowned."

"So," Mihalis took up the story, "a sailor will vow to build a church if his life is saved."

"And that's why they have three hundred churches!" Bert said with a chuckle. "But why the Church of the Cat?"

"One sailor didn't have much money. He hadn't said how big a church he'd build so he made a very small one, only about two feet high, and nailed it to the roof of his house!" Mihalis went on. "The first day after it was built a cat moved in! It's been called the Church of the Cat ever since!"

"That's a good story," Bert said with a grin.

"Maybe we should build a church for Snoop," Freddie said.

"Let's make one when we get home!" Flossie proposed.

The Church of the Cat proved to be just around the corner. It looked like a doll house perched up on the roof.

"Now we'll go to the waterfront to see Omega, Irene, and Peter," Mihalis said when the twins had admired the little church.

"Are they friends of yours?" Nan asked.

Aliki began to giggle. When Flossie wanted to know what the matter was, the little Greek girl only laughed harder.

"You're not being polite," Mihalis scolded her, but he began to laugh too.

Finally Aliki managed to say between giggles, "They're pelicans!"

The Bobbseys all laughed too, then Freddie cried, "I want to see them!"

The six children ran down the narrow lane which led toward the waterfront. After a short distance the lane widened into a little square.

Aliki looked around. "This is where the shop is that sells *amygdalota!*" she exclaimed. "I'm going to buy some!" She ran into a doorway. In a few minutes Aliki returned with a white box which she passed around to the others.

"Take some," she urged. "They're cakes made of almonds and honey, and you can buy them only on Mykonos!"

"Ooh, they're yummy!" Flossie cried as she bit into one of the sweets.

"There are our friends!" Mihalis said teasingly as they reached the waterfront. He pointed to three large white birds with very long bills.

"Which one is Irene?" Nan asked.

Mihalis shook his head. "I'm not sure," he said. "But I think that pelican standing on one leg is Peter. He's the crossest."

"I'm going to give him a cake," Freddie declared. He picked one from the box and walked toward the strange-looking bird. He held out his hand with the cake. The pelican carefully took the morsel and clucked gratefully.

"He likes it!" Freddie cried gleefully. "I'll give him another!"

"They're gone." Aliki showed him the empty box.

"It's time we began our climb back anyhow," Mihalis spoke up.

With the Greek boy to guide them, the children made the return trip to the Pappas house without getting lost in the town's crooked streets. After lunch and a rest during the hottest part of the day the youngsters walked down again to meet Stefanos for the trip to Delos. Mr. and

"He likes it!" Freddie cried gleefully

Mrs. Bobbsey had decided to stay on the terrace with their host and hostess.

Stefanos was waiting when the children ran onto the pier. "How long will it take to get to Delos?" Bert asked as he stepped aboard the launch.

"We should make it in less than an hour with a calm sea," Stefanos replied. "The return trip takes longer because we will be going against the wind."

The children could see several other small islands during the ride. They were all brown and very sparsely settled.

"The tourists are more interested in the stone lions on Delos than in anything else," Stefanos told his passengers.

"Lions?" Freddie opened his eyes wide. "I want to see them!"

"Why are they on Delos?" Nan asked curiously.

Stefanos replied that the lions had been set up to guard the Sacred Way to the Temple of Apollo. "And they're still standing there after twenty-six hundred years!" he concluded.

By this time the launch had been tied up to a small dock. The children jumped out and followed the skipper. The flat brown island seemed to be covered with broken stone. When Stefanos explained that these stones had been the foundations of ancient buildings, the children became very interested.

They listened as he described the city which had been so busy and prosperous before its destruction thousands of years before. He showed them mosaics which had been uncovered by archaeologists. Nan was particularly fascinated by these pictures made of tiny pieces of colored stone.

But Freddie was still thinking about the lions. He wandered away from the others and walked up onto a little rise. From here he could see the water all around him, and in the distance some large white objects gleamed.

"The lions!" he thought excitedly and began to run toward them.

As he came nearer he saw there were five of the huge stone beasts. Seated on stone pedestals, they seemed to be still guarding the ruins.

"I'll get Flossie to take my picture with one of them!" Freddie decided and started back toward the spot where Stefanos and the other children were standing.

At that moment he saw something near the water which attracted his attention. Two men were digging in the sand. "Maybe they're archaeologists!" he thought excitedly. He stood still and watched.

The men lifted a heavy object from the hole

they had dug and staggered toward a small blue motorboat pulled up onto the sand nearby. The next minute Freddie saw them place the object in the boat. They shoved the craft into the water and jumped in. The motor started up, and the boat sped off.

"That's funny" Freddie thought. "Those men acted sneaky!" He ran up to Stefanos and the other children and described what he had seen.

"They were stealing something from the government!" Flossie cried immediately. "Let's chase them!"

"Now wait a minute!" Bert said teasingly. "Aren't you going a little fast?"

"Flossie may be right," Nan said. "You remember Mr. Gorzako told us antiquities were being taken from Delos!"

By this time the others were excited too. They urged Stefanos to follow the blue boat. Smilingly he agreed and they all dashed down to the launch. The skipper cast off and headed away from the island.

Through his binoculars Stefanos spotted the blue boat in the distance. "They seem to be going toward Mykonos," he reported. "They have a fast boat, and it's hard to see against the blue water."

"Oh, we must catch them!" Flossie insisted.

"We will do our best!" Stefanos promised.

But the blue boat had a good head start. It skimmed over the water. Several times the launch lost it among the tiny islands which dotted the sea.

Finally, after a half hour, the launch gained on the motorboat. The children took turns peering through the binoculars.

"There are two men, all right," Bert reported. "One of them has on a tan cap and the other some kind of round black hat. They keep looking back here. I think they know they're being followed!"

"They'll probably run up on the beach at Mykonos," Stefanos guessed. "We'll have to put in at the dock, but you boys can jump off and get someone to stop the men."

"Bert and I will get them for sure!" Freddie boasted.

They were nearing the crescent-shaped harbor when suddenly Bert cried out:

"The blue boat has disappeared!"

CHAPTER XVI

THE HIDDEN COVE

"THE blue boat gone! How could it be?" Mihalis shouted, grabbing the glasses and scanning the water ahead of them. "It was just over there to the left of the harbor a minute ago."

Everyone looked through the glasses, but the blue boat was not in sight. Finally Stefanos gave up and headed for the dock.

Next morning after breakfast the children decided to go into town. "I'd like to buy something special to take to Nellie," Nan declared.

"And I want something for Susie Larker," Flossie spoke up. Susie was Flossie's best friend in Lakeport.

"Also," said Bert eagerly, "we can keep our eyes peeled for those men we were chasing yesterday."

The six children made their way down through the narrow winding streets until they came to the area of shops. It was difficult to tell the shops from the private houses. Both were built of white stone and opened on the street.

"All the buildings look so clean!" Nan said admiringly.

"They're whitewashed once a year," Mihalis explained.

The youngsters walked into a shop where woven skirts and other articles were displayed. From a small room in the rear came the *thump, thump, thump* of a hand loom. An elderly woman arose from her weaving and greeted them with a smile.

Nan and Flossie walked around the room admiring the bright clothes. Nan picked out a pretty hand-woven belt for Nellie. Flossie bought Susie a tiny doll in native costume.

In another shop Nan held up a bag woven in colored stripes. "Isn't this pretty?" she said. "It looks like the one Petros had on Parnassus."

"They are very popular with American ladies," the shopkeeper told her.

"Let's buy one for Mother!" Nan proposed. The other twins thought this was a good idea. A quick count of the money in their pockets produced enough for the purchase. Nan swung the bag over her shoulder and they continued down the street. They paused once more for Bert to buy a tie for Charlie Mason while Freddie got a wooden whistle for his pal Teddy Blake. Then they found themselves in a tiny square. A man stood there reading a letter.

"Look at him!" Freddie whispered to Bert.

The man was rather plump and wore a round, black fur hat. His thick black eyebrows met over his little beady eyes.

"That's one of the men in the boat we chased from Delos yesterday!" Freddie declared.

"And I'll bet he's Thanos!" Bert stated. "But what's he doing here?"

Nan had a sudden hunch. "Maybe he's also in the gang that's stealing antiquities!" she said.

The man looked up quickly. He seemed to realize the children were discussing him. He stuffed the letter into his pocket and hurried off down a side street.

"I'd like to talk to him!" Bert declared and began to run after the man. The others followed.

Reaching the next corner they saw the suspect hastening along the flagstone alley. He looked back over his shoulder, then increased his pace to a run. The children speeded up.

A few minutes later they met a man on a motorcycle and had to squeeze against the wall to let him pass. When they took up their chase again the fugitive was some distance ahead. He seemed familiar with the twisting and turning alleys and did not slacken his pace.

Finally, the children turned a corner. There was no sign of the plump man. They halted, discouraged.

"We've lost him," Nan said with a sigh. "We might as well go back to the shops."

Mihalis looked embarrassed. "I don't like to say this," he admitted, "but I'm not sure which direction to take."

"We're lost!" Flossie wailed. "How will we get back?"

"There's one way I've heard about, but I don't know whether it will work," said Mihalis.

The Greek boy explained that the old-timers on the island always said that if you walked into the wind you would eventually reach the harbor.

"But wind blows from different directions," Nan objected.

"Not the *meltemi*," Aliki spoke up. "It always blows from the north. That's what makes the island cool in the summer."

"Okay, let's find the wind," Bert agreed.

But this was not an easy thing to do. The crooked and confusing streets prevented the wind from penetrating very far from the water-front.

The children walked around and around, on the alert for a breeze which would set them in the right direction. Finally Nan turned a corner ahead of the others. "I feel it!" she called back. "The wind is blowing up this street!"

They all hurried after her. This lane proved to be fairly straight with only a few bends. As they walked along it, the children could feel the breeze growing stronger. Another turn and they could see the blue sea at the end of the street!

"The wind saved us!" Flossie cried, her cheeks pink with excitement. "It found us when we were lost!"

The children came out onto the wide, paved area by the harbor. At the same time they saw two men hurrying toward a blue motorboat which had been pulled up onto the strip of sand. One was the man with the round fur hat!

"Stop!" Bert yelled. "Stop!"

The man looked back, spoke to his companion, and the two raced onto the beach. The three pelicans were crouched at the edge of the sand. As the man with the black hat dashed past, Peter reached out his long bill and nipped the fugitive's hand.

The man cried out angrily and jumped into the boat. His companion shoved it into the water, started the engine, and the two men roared off.

"Isn't there some way we can follow them?" Bert asked desperately.

Mihalis looked around. There was a rowboat on the sand. He spoke quickly in Greek with an old fisherman nearby.

"It's this man's boat," Mihalis reported. "He says we may borrow it."

"We can't all get in," Aliki observed. "I'll stay here with Freddie and Flossie."

The small twins looked disappointed, but they could see there was not enough room in the boat.

"All right," Freddie agreed. "I'm sure I could help catch him though!"

"You've helped a lot already," Bert said consolingly. "You were the one who saw him first!"

Hurriedly the older children climbed into the boat. Bert and Mihalis took up the oars, and the old fisherman pushed the craft out into the water.

"Which way did the men go?" Bert asked, scanning the small harbor.

"Over to the left," Nan replied. "They're not in sight. They must have gone around that point."

The two boys rowed strongly across the harbor and around the point.

"Where *is* that blue boat?" Nan said, bewildered, looking around. "I'm sure it came this way!"

"Maybe they've landed," Bert suggested.

The boys turned the boat toward shore and rowed along parallel to it. Here and there white houses dotted the hilly landscape. The three children carefully studied the shoreline. There was no sign of a motorboat.

"But they couldn't just vanish!" Bert said, puzzled.

Mihalis looked thoughtful. "Perhaps there's a

passage in between some of these rocks," he suggested.

The boys slowly rowed as close to the shore as they could. At this point the sandy beach had disappeared. Huge rocky cliffs rose straight up from the water.

Nan peered intently at the rocks. "I think I see an opening!" she called out presently. "It's very narrow. I don't know whether a boat can get in there or not."

Mihalis took both oars while Bert slid to the seat beside Nan. They directed the Greek boy toward the slit in the rocks.

"You can just about make it!" Bert encouraged.

Mihalis brought the boat to the mouth of the opening. Then he pulled in both oars. The rocky sides of the passage were straight and high. The boat just cleared them.

The three children stood up in the craft and placed their hands against the rocks. Then carefully they pushed the boat along the narrow channel.

"How far does this go?" Nan panted. Her hands were getting sore from rubbing against the rough stone.

Mihalis grinned back at her. "Not much farther," he called. "I can see a cove just ahead."

A minute later the passage widened and the rowboat came out into a small bay. On the

The three children stood up and placed their hands
against the rocks

seaward side were the high rocks, while the other three sides were steep slopes covered with scraggly trees and low bushes.

"There's the men's boat!" Bert pointed out.

The blue craft was at the far side of the cove, tied to a tree close to the water's edge.

"But where are the men?" Nan asked in surprise.

There was no sign of the boat's occupants and no movement among the bushes. Nan shivered. "It's spooky!" she said in a low voice.

"Let's get out and look around," Bert suggested.

Mihalis spotted a small beach to one side. He rowed to it and the three climbed out.

"We'd better hide our boat in case the men come back," Bert declared.

Nearby was a large clump of bushes. The children pulled the rowboat up as far behind the bushes as they could manage.

"It's not entirely out of sight, but I guess it's the best we can do," Mihalis said as he straightened up. "What do we do now?"

"Try to climb up to the top," Bert proposed.

At that moment there came the sound of men's voices from the other side of the cove. They seemed to be growing louder and louder.

"Oh!" Nan gasped and looked around. "Someone's coming!" she whispered excitedly. "Where can we hide?"

CHAPTER XVII

"FOLLOW THAT CAR!"

"QUICK!" Bert hissed. "We can hide here!" He pulled Nan down behind a thick bush. Mihalis crouched beside them.

"The men are on the other side of the cove. They won't spot us!" he said.

Soon the children could see two men, one plump and one tall, slipping and sliding down the hillside. They were lugging a heavy bundle. The pair headed for the beached motorboat, and dumped their burden into it. Then they both sank down on the sand to rest.

Nan peeped cautiously around the bush. "The one in the fur hat is the man we think is Thanos!"

The steep walls of the cove carried the men's conversation clearly to the ears of the three in hiding. The men spoke in Greek, which Mihalis translated in whispers. "The plump man with the fur hat *is* Thanos," he told the twins. "The other one has been working on Delos for some archaeologists."

Nan and Bert waited tensely while Mihalis listened again. "Flossie was right!" he whispered excitedly. "The man from Delos stole a huge marble foot which had been excavated. He hid the foot in the sand on Delos until Thanos could come for it."

"They're the men Freddie spotted," said Nan.

"Yes," Mihalis added. "And the tall man has stolen other valuable relics and sold them to Thanos."

There was a short silence while the men stretched their arms. Then Mihalis continued his translation. "They did know we were following them yesterday. They had intended to take the marble foot to *The Bull,* which is anchored down the coast a short distance."

"They didn't want to lead us to *The Bull,*" Bert guessed, "so they came in here. That's why we lost them."

Mihalis nodded. "Right. They hid their loot in some bushes on the hillside. Now they're planning to take it to *The Bull,* which is going back to Piraeus this afternoon."

"We can't let them get away!" Nan said desperately.

"We can get Stefanos to take us home this afternoon, too," Mihalis declared.

"Yes, we must!" Bert agreed. He peeked through the bushes again. The men were still stretched out on the beach. "If there were only some way we could get out of here now!"

The men appeared to be in no hurry to leave. The children's legs were getting stiff from their cramped positions. They stirred uneasily. Finally, after a long time, Thanos sat up. He poked his companion, who appeared to have fallen asleep.

The tall man got up slowly, and the two jumped into their boat. In a few minutes they had left the cove.

The children waited until they thought the men had gone through the narrow channel. Then they put their own boat into the water and rowed away.

When they reached the water front at Mykonos and beached the rowboat, they found Aliki and the younger twins playing with a kitten in front of one of the shops.

"Did you catch them?" Freddie asked at once.

Bert and Nan told the younger children about the thieves and the marble foot which they were planning to take back to Piraeus in *The Bull*.

"Can't we follow them?" Flossie wanted to know.

Mihalis told her that he thought Stefanos could take the party back to Piraeus that afternoon. "We'll ask your parents and Mr. and Mrs. Pappas if it will be all right," he proposed.

The six children made their way up to the Pappas house and told the grownups about their morning's adventures. Mr. Bobbsey agreed to the plan of returning to the mainland that afternoon.

Mr. Pappas reached Stefanos at the small hotel where he was staying in town. He said he would be ready to start for Piraeus within an hour.

Then Mihalis and Bert put in a call to Mr. Gorzako at his office. When they told him about the stolen marble from Delos, he agreed to notify the police at Piraeus.

"They can be watching for *The Bull* when it comes in," he told the boys.

"We'll have a light lunch on the terrace," Mrs. Pappas suggested. "Costa will be here with his taxis to take you all to the dock by the time you've eaten."

So, with everyone hurrying, the Bobbsey party was on board the Gorzako launch and speeding out of the harbor in a short time.

Mrs. Bobbsey sat down in the chair next to Nan. "What a pretty bag," she said. "I've been noticing it for some time but haven't had a chance to ask you about it."

Flossie had been listening. Before Nan could reply she cried out, "We bought it for you, Mommy! It's like the one the goat boy had!"

Nan laughed as she handed the woven pouch to her mother. "So many exciting things have happened," she said, "that I forgot I was carrying it! We all bought this for you in Mykonos."

"You dear children!" Mrs. Bobbsey exclaimed. "Your father and I bought you all some things too, but you'll have to wait until we get home to see them. I had them mailed to Lakeport!"

"Please tell us what they are, Mommy!" Flossie pleaded. But her mother only smiled and shook her head.

The children spent most of the long ride back to the mainland peering at all the fishing boats which they passed but did not see *The Bull*.

"I'm afraid they've given us the slip somehow," Bert said in a worried tone.

It was early evening when Stefanos reached the Gorzako dock in Piraeus. Etsi and the bus were there to meet them. Their friend was talking to a tall policeman.

Etsi ran up to take the luggage and stow it in the bus. "This policeman tells me they have men stationed all along the harbor looking for *The Bull* but it hasn't come in yet," he said.

"Your mother and I will wait in the car," Mr. Bobbsey said to the twins. "You children walk up and down if you like, but don't get too far away."

"Freddie and Flossie and I will walk up this way," Bert said, "and Nan, you go the other way with Mihalis and Aliki. Whoever spots *The Bull* first can call out."

Freddie and Flossie ran up the pavement which skirted the harbor, staring at the names of the boats tied up there. The vessels were from all parts of the world. Bert followed slowly, reading the names of the home ports which were painted on the bows of the ships.

"New York, Cairo, Tripoli, Naples," he said to himself as he walked along.

Suddenly Flossie came running back toward him. "Look!" she cried, pointing to a battered-looking old fishing vessel which was just docking. "Isn't that the funny name we're looking for?"

Bert peered at the name on the peeling hull. It was ΒΥΛΛ

"That's it!" Bert cried excitedly. "Come on!" With Freddie and Flossie at his heels he ran back to the bus and Etsi. The policeman hurried up.

"You've seen it?" he asked.

Freddie showed him as Nan and the Greek children joined the group. At that moment an old car sped up to the dock and stopped. A plump man with a fur hat dashed from the deck of *The Bull*. He ran over a plank which had

"Look!" cried Flossie. "Isn't that the funny name
we're looking for?"

been pushed out between the fishing boat and the pier. He carried a heavy bundle and one hand was bandaged. Quickly he jumped into the waiting car, which immediately started up.

"It's Thanos!" Bert yelled. "Follow that car!"

He and the other children piled into the bus. Etsi spun around and drove off in pursuit. As he did, a car with four policemen in it swung in behind them.

"Good!" Mr. Bobbsey said in relief. "The police are with us!"

The old car sped up the street with Etsi and the police car following. A mile or so beyond the dock the first car turned up a steep street. It went for a block, then turned into the open door of a shabby-looking garage. The door closed behind it.

Etsi parked the bus across the street and waited for the police. The four officers jumped from their car. The one in charge pounded on the door of the garage and called out in Greek.

After a few minutes the door opened. One of the policemen beckoned to the children. They jumped from the bus and followed the officers into the building.

Inside was a room which seemed to be used as a warehouse. It was almost entirely filled with large bales.

There were two men in the room. One was Thanos and the other Dimitris, the man who had let them into the fur factory on Crete.

"Are these the men you suspect?" the officer in charge asked Bert.

The boy nodded. "The one with the fur hat is the one we think stole Mr. Karilis' fur and his truck."

The officer spoke to the men in Greek. They both glared at the children and burst into a flood of words and gestures.

"They insist they're fur workers," the officer said. Pointing toward the bales, he went on, "The bales are finished fur plates ready to be shipped to America. They may be telling the truth, but we'll look around."

The policemen fanned out through the room, peering behind the bales. They found nothing suspicious.

Nan strolled around after them, trying to read the labels on some of the bales. As she walked past a desk against one wall she looked down. There, scattered on the desk top, were several stiff white labels, a small pot of black ink, and a brush.

"They look like the label we found in the hat in Mr. Karilis' fur shop at home," she thought. Suddenly her eyes caught something else.

There was a plain label with a drawing of the

bull's horns and two Greek words: *tessera okto!*

Nan's heart raced. This was where the strange label had come from! She picked up the piece of paper and started toward the police officer. But Dimitris had been watching her. He hurried across the room, grabbed the label from her hand, tore it into little pieces and tossed the pieces into the wastebasket!

Nan opened her mouth to protest. But before she could say anything there came a cry from one corner of the room. It was Freddie.

"I see something important!" he exclaimed.

CHAPTER XVIII

"EFCHARISTO, BOBBSEYS!"

AT Freddie's cry everyone in the old garage turned to look at him. He was peering at a bale of fur which stood behind several others in the corner.

"What do you see, Freddie?" Bert asked.

Breathlessly Freddie pointed to a long slit in the bale. "Something white's hidden inside!" he cried.

One of the policemen grabbed a knife from the desk and quickly slashed open the bale. A large marble foot slid onto the floor!

"So you did steal this!" the officer cried, whirling around toward Thanos and Dimitris. The men were not there!

"They must have sneaked out the door," Mihalis guessed.

"I'll get them!" Bert shouted and dashed outside. He looked up and down the street. The two men were just disappearing around a corner to his right.

"Stop!" he yelled, racing up the street after them. Two policemen followed.

The fugitives continued to run while several passersby paused and stared curiously. The men were drawing farther away when suddenly they were forced to slow down at a crossroad.

An elderly man was trudging along a steep side street, pushing a cart piled high with vegetables. The peddler reached the intersection at the same moment as the fleeing men. To avoid a collision they attempted to swerve around the cart.

The second's delay was enough for Bert. Seizing the opportunity, he threw himself forward in a flying tackle, grabbing Thanos around the ankles. They both fell to the ground with a crash!

The policemen were right behind Bert. One of them grabbed Thanos, pulled him to his feet, and began to march him back to the garage.

When Thanos had fallen, Dimitris hesitated briefly before resuming his flight. But the second policeman plunged after him and ordered the thin man to halt. With a shrug the fugitive surrendered.

Mr. and Mrs. Bobbsey and the other children were standing in front of the garage as the procession came down the street. "Good for you, Bert!" Mihalis called. "You caught the thieves!"

Bert threw himself forward in a flying tackle

"Not by myself," Bert said modestly.

The policemen smiled at him. "They probably would have escaped if you hadn't acted as quickly as you did," one said.

Bert grinned. "We've chased Thanos so often I *had* to help catch him this time!"

The police padlocked the garage and led the two men away to jail. Etsi drove his passengers on to the Gorzako home. Here, over a late dinner, the twins told their hosts the story of their adventures.

Mihalis and Aliki were jubilant at their American friends' success in solving the mystery.

Aliki gave a huge sigh. "You are the most exciting guests we've ever had," she said.

"Indeed they are!" Mr. Gorzako chuckled.

"Now maybe the king won't lose any more statues," Flossie spoke up.

Everyone laughed. Mrs. Gorzako hugged the little girl. "I'm sure he'll be very grateful!" she declared.

The next morning Mr. Gorzako received a call from the police asking if the Bobbsey children would come down to headquarters and officially identify the prisoners.

When they walked into the chief's office, Mr. Yannis Karilis jumped up from a chair. He rushed over and embraced the children.

"You have found my fur!" he cried. "Now all

my people have work again. My brother will be
so happy! How can we ever thank you?"

"We like being detectives," Freddie spoke up
after he had recovered from his embarrassment
at being hugged. "We had fun!"

"Well, you seem to have solved two puzzling
mysteries," the chief said. "I'm going to have
Thanos and Dimitris brought in here so you can
hear the whole story."

The two sullen prisoners were led into the
room. Under questioning by the chief, they admitted that they were members of a large ring of
thieves. Yannis translated the conversation for
the Bobbseys.

"You stole the bale of fur from Mr. Karilis,
didn't you?" the police officer said, looking
sternly at Thanos.

"Sure!" Thanos admitted defiantly. "We gave
work to our people on Crete. They sewed the bits
of fur into plates."

"He means those big pieces of fur," Freddie
whispered to his twin.

"I *know,* Freddie," Flossie replied impatiently.

The chief turned to Dimitris, who was chew-
ing his mustache nervously. "And *you* concen-
trated on stealing antiquities!" he said accus-
ingly.

"Greece is full of old statues," Dimitris

replied harshly. "The government doesn't need them all. I helped myself to those I could find."

"And you shipped them out of the country concealed in the bales of finished fur," the officer continued.

"We were pretty smart!" Dimitris boasted. "We got money for both the fur and the antiquities that way!"

"Ask him if he dug up the little bronze chariot that Nan saw in the pit on Crete," Flossie suggested.

Yannis put the question, then translated Dimitris' reply. "He says he was digging around near the Palace of Knossos thinking he might find something. He did dig up the chariot, but he was afraid the guard had seen him. So he wrapped it in his handkerchief and dropped it into the pit planning to come back for it later. He is very angry that you found it!"

"Did he have anything to do with the disappearing statue of Pan on Mount Parnassus?" Bert asked excitedly.

This time in answer to Yannis's question, there was a flood of explanations from both Dimitris and Thanos. The two had driven the truck to Delphi to hunt for any marble statues which they might be able to find.

On the outskirts of the town they had swerved

to avoid some fallen rock and had wrecked the truck. They had not been hurt, and continued their quest. The men's next move was to buy two donkeys, saying they were artists planning a sketching trip through the mountains.

"Did they dig up the statue of Pan in the big cave?" Nan wanted to know.

"Thanos says they had heard the story that the cave was sacred to Pan," Mr. Karilis said, "and so had hoped there would be a statue of the god there. When they found it, they left it in the smaller cave until they could take it away the next morning. Dimitris played a flute to frighten people away from the mountain."

"And also toppled Petros' hut and left the warning note?" Nan put in.

"Yes."

"Then Dimitris and Thanos must have picked up a car somewhere and taken the statue across the gulf on the ferry," Bert surmised.

There was another short conversation in Greek. "That's right," Yannis said. "They bought an old car in a village beyond Delphi." Then he smiled as he continued. "Dimitris says he lost the ferry ticket he had bought in Athens and had to buy another!"

"That's the ticket Bert found in the truck!" Nan said triumphantly.

"And they were the men who grabbed that bronze head away from Nan on the beach!" Freddie cried.

"But I thought Thanos had gone out on *The Bull* two days before," Bert said, puzzled.

The chief asked Thanos for an explanation. He said the skipper of *The Bull* had received storm warnings and so had not left port. Thanos and Dimitris were on their way to the boat when they spied the helmeted head on the beach. Dimitris had taken it to the garage after Thanos had sailed.

When the prisoners had been led from the room the chief stood up. He shook hands with each of the Bobbsey twins. "We are glad you came to Greece," he said formally. "You have solved two very troublesome mysteries for us."

"We're glad we came to Greece too!" the four children chorused as they waved good-by.

That evening Mr. Bobbsey announced that they would leave Athens in three days for the return flight to America. The next days were busy ones, filled with sightseeing and last-minute shopping.

The day before they were to leave, Mr. Yannis Karilis appeared at the Gorzako home to see the twins. He carried four round boxes which he gave them.

Flossie tore the lid off hers. "It's a fur hat!" she cried in delight.

Quickly the others pulled out identical hats. When they had finished trying them on and thanking him, Yannis said, "I told my workers that you found the fur bale. So the first things they made were hats for you! They are very grateful!"

As Yannis was about to leave, Nan spoke up. "We never found out about those labels with the mark of bull's horns and the Greek words," she said. "And that was the beginning of the mystery back in Lakeport."

"I'll try to get the answer to your question, Nan," Yannis promised. "I'll call you."

He telephoned late that evening. Yannis had gone to the jail to talk to Dimitris. "He told me that the bull's horns were the symbol of the gang because most of the members came from Crete. That's also the reason they called their boat *The Bull*. The numbers were the dates of the next shipment of the bales containing the antiquities."

"Was Mr. Andreas Karilis' foreman a member of the gang?" Nan asked.

"Yes. He was their contact in America. He would always receive the bales and take out the smuggled antiquities before my brother saw them. It was just by chance that Andreas opened the carton of fur hats and you found the note."

"Now everything is explained," Nan said happily. "We'll tell your brother all about it when we get back to Lakeport."

"Also tell him I think American children are very smart!" Yannis said. "For both of us, efcharisto to the Bobbseys!"

The next day as the Bobbseys were saying good-by to the Gorzakos before leaving for the airport, the two Greek children stepped forward. Each held two long, narrow boxes. Aliki handed one each to Nan and Flossie, and Mihalis gave his to Bert and Freddie.

"Don't open these until you're on the plane," Aliki directed, smiling mysteriously.

Later, the giant jet plane carrying the Bobbseys rose into the air. Immediately Flossie opened her box and the others did the same. In each box lay a string of beautiful worry beads!

"Goody!" said Flossie. She picked up the beads and began to click them along on the string. "Now I'll never worry again!"